HER PERMANENT RECORD

MEET THE GANG!

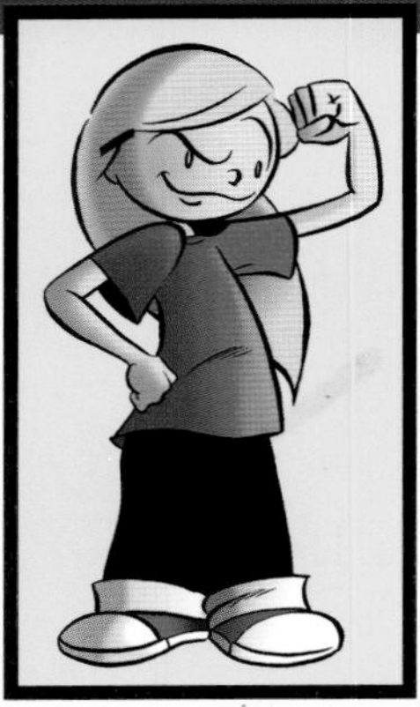

Amelia Louise McBride:
Our heroine. Wise cracking, yet sweet. She spends her time hanging out with friends and her aunt Tanner.

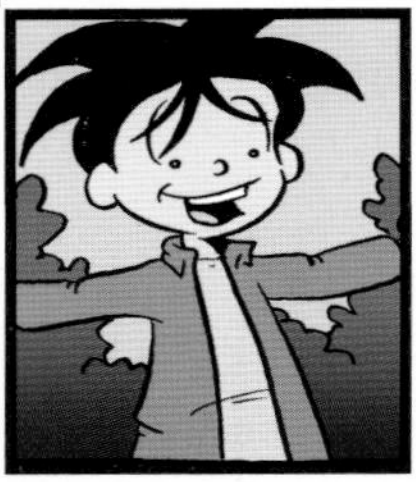

Reggie Grabinsky:
A.k.a. Captain Amazing. Founder of G.A.S.P., which he forces . . . er, encourages, his friends to join.

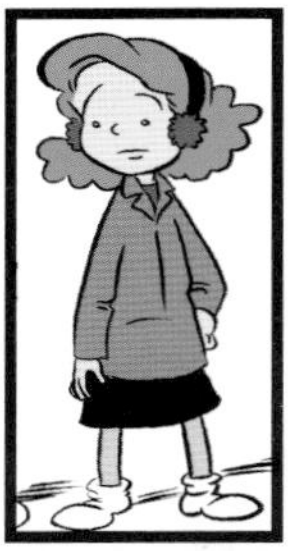

Rhonda Bleenie:
Smart, stubborn, and loud. She wears her heart on her sleeve and it's filled with love for Reggie.

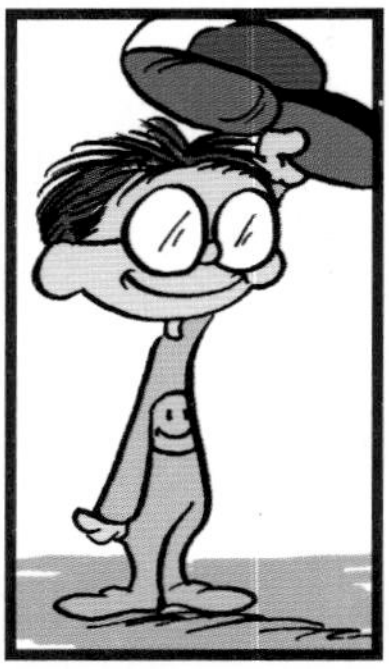

Pajamaman:
Never speaks. Always cool. His feetie jammies tell you what's on his mind.

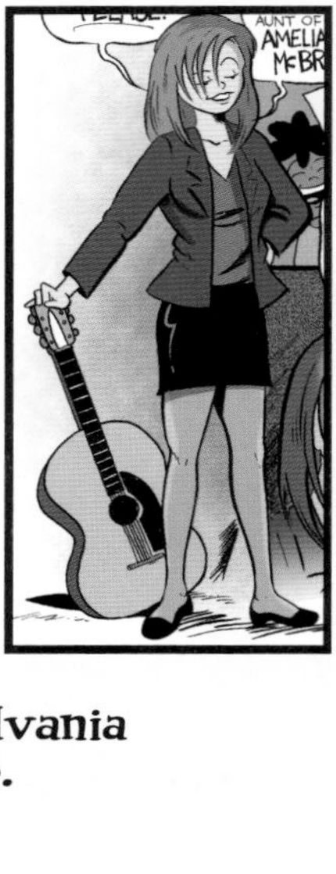
AUNT OF
AMELIA

Tanner:
Amelia's aunt and a former rock 'n' roll superstar.

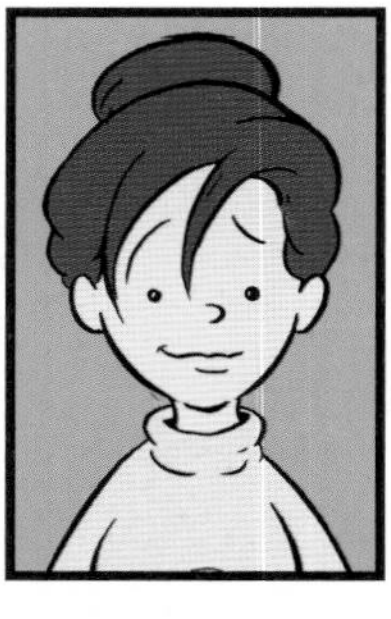

Amelia's Mom (Mary):
Starting a new life in Pennsylvania with Amelia after the divorce.

Amelia's Dad:
Still lives in New York, and misses Amelia terribly.

G.A.S.P.
Gathering Of Awesome Super Pals. The superhero club Reggie founded.

Park View Terrace Ninjas:
Club across town and nemesis to G.A.S.P.

Kyle:
The main ninja. Kind of a jerk but not without charm.

Joan:
Former Park View Terrace Ninja (nemesis of G.A.S.P.), now friends with Amelia and company.

Tweenie Zeenie:
A local kid-run magazine and Web site.

Jimmy Gownley's

AMELIA RULES!™

HER PERMANENT RECORD

A Atheneum Books for Young Readers
atheneum New York London Toronto Sydney New Delhi

ATHENEUM BOOKS FOR YOUNG READERS
An imprint of Simon & Schuster Children's Publishing Division
1230 Avenue of the Americas, New York, New York 10020

ATHENEUM BOOKS FOR YOUNG READERS is a registered trademark of Simon & Schuster, Inc.
Atheneum logo is a trademark of Simon & Schuster, Inc.
For information about special discounts for bulk purchases, please contact Simon & Schuster Special Sales at 1-866-506-1949 or business@simonandschuster.com.
The Simon & Schuster Speakers Bureau can bring authors to your live event. For more information or to book an event, contact the Simon & Schuster Speakers Bureau at 1-866-248-3049 or visit our website at www.simonspeakers.com.
Also available in an Atheneum Books for Young Readers hardcover edition.
Book design by Sonia Chaghatzbanian
The text for this book is hand-lettered.
The illustrations for this book are digitally rendered.
Manufactured in China
0712 GFC
First Edition
2 4 6 8 10 9 7 5 3 1
Library of Congress Cataloging-in-Publication Data
Gownley, Jimmy.
Her permanent record / Jimmy Gownley ; [illustrated by] Jimmy Gownley. — 1st ed.
p. cm. — (Jimmy Gownley's Amelia rules ; [18])
ISBN 978-1-4169-8615-7 (hardcover)
ISBN 978-1-4169-8614-0 (paperback)
1. Graphic novels. [1. Graphic novels. 2. Voyages and travels—Fiction. 3. Aunts—Fiction. 4. Friendship—Fiction. 5. Schools—Fiction.] I. Title.
PZ7.7.G69Her 2012
741.5'973—dc23   2011053039

This book is dedicated with love
to Karen, Anna, and Stella.

HER PERMANENT RECORD

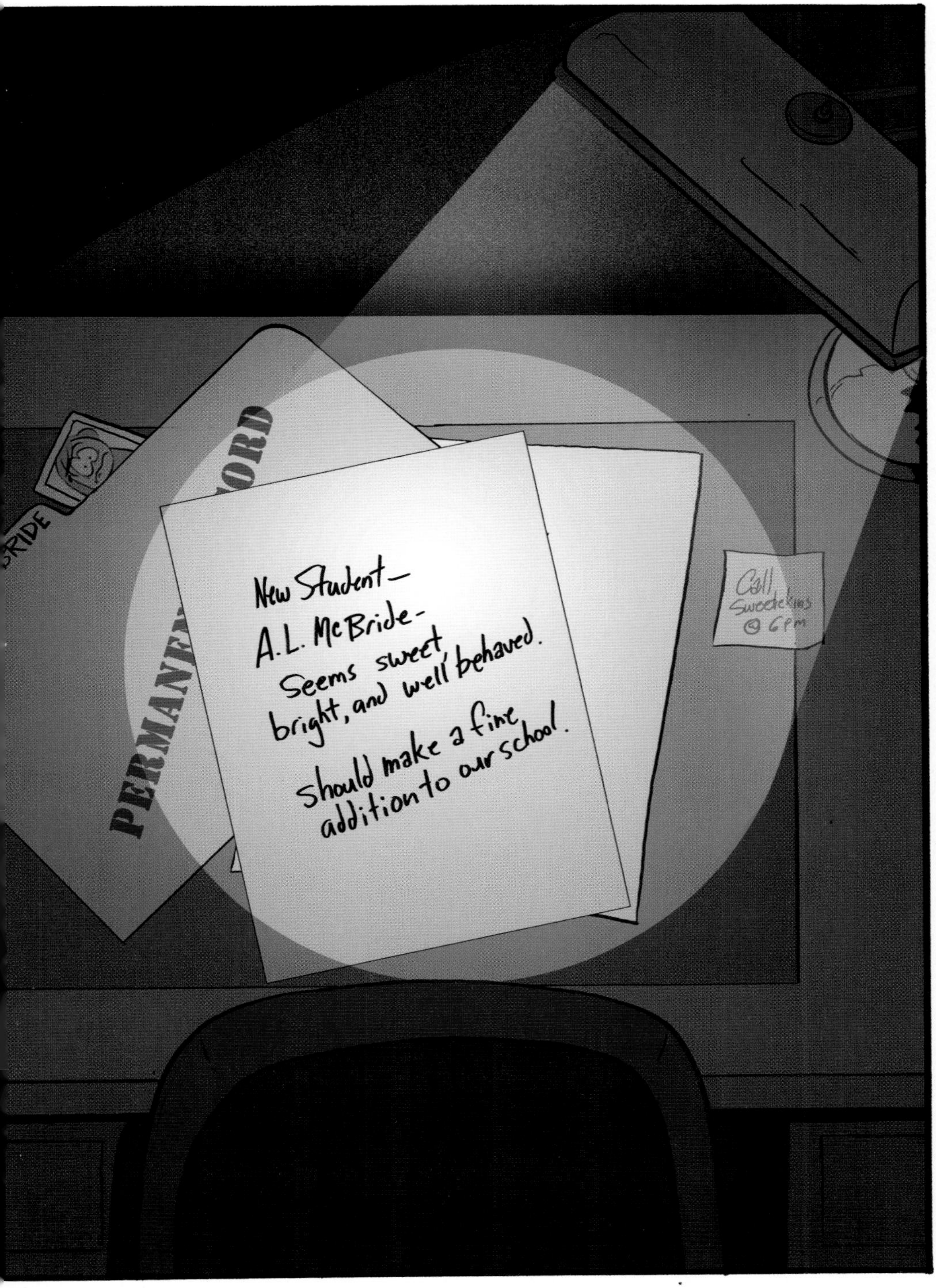
RIDE
PERMANE
ORD
New Student—
A.L. McBride-
Seems sweet,
bright, and well behaved.
Should make a fine
addition to our school.
Call
Sweetekins
@ 6pm

AMELIA RULES!™

SO...
...WHO IS AMELIA LOUISE McBRIDE, ANYWAY?
AND WHAT, *EXACTLY*, IS GOING TO END UP ON HER PERMANENT RECORD?
WELL...
...THAT'S A *GOOD QUESTION.*

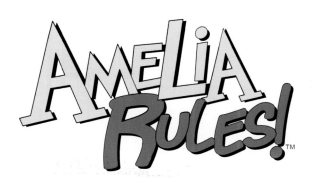

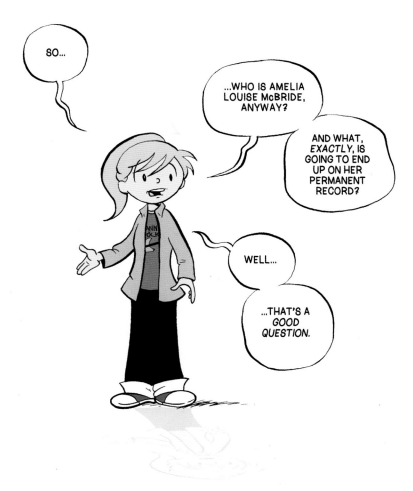

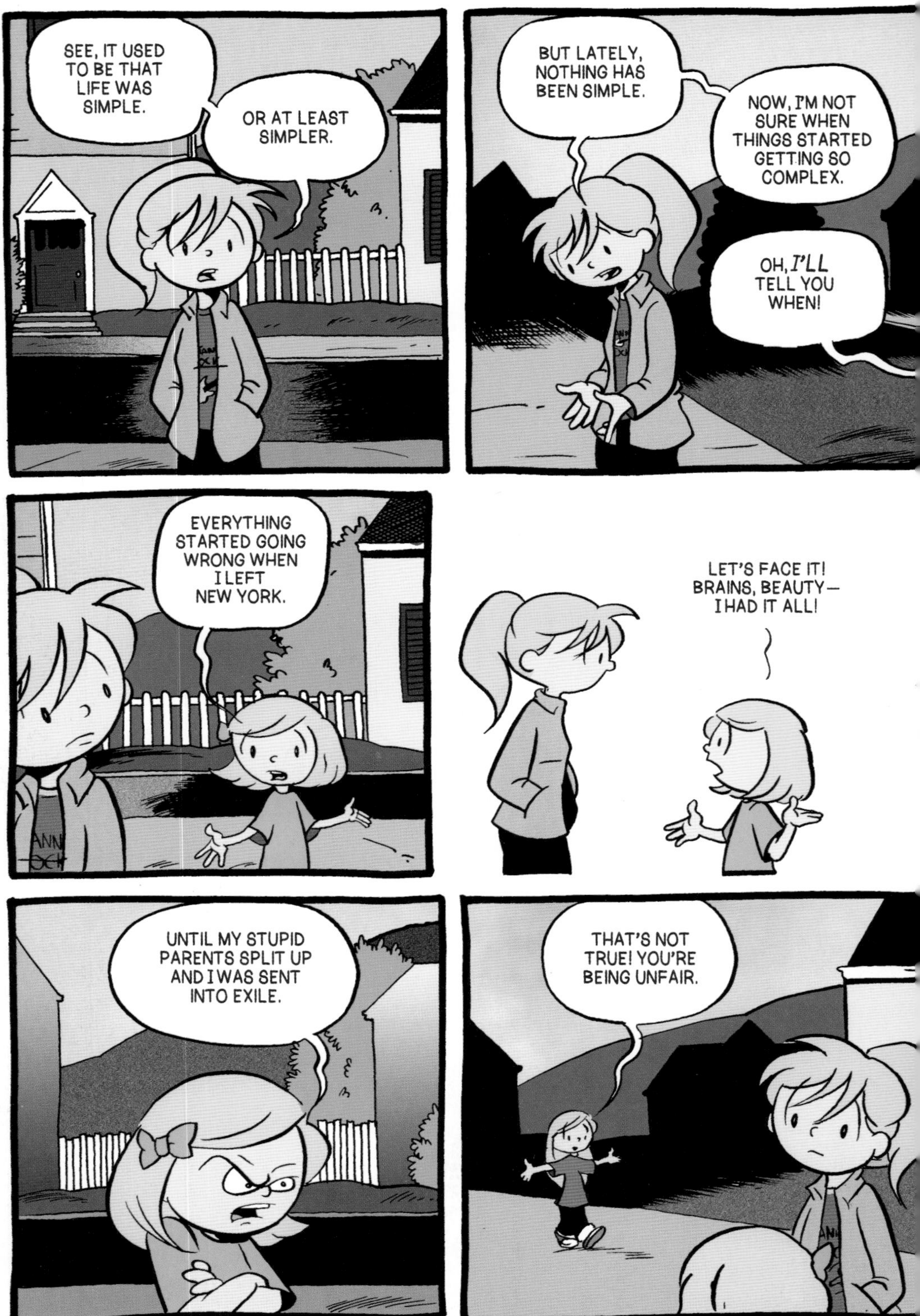
SEE, IT USED TO BE THAT LIFE WAS SIMPLE.
OR AT LEAST SIMPLER.
BUT LATELY, NOTHING HAS BEEN SIMPLE.
NOW, I'M NOT SURE WHEN THINGS STARTED GETTING SO COMPLEX.
OH, *I'LL* TELL YOU WHEN!
EVERYTHING STARTED GOING WRONG WHEN I LEFT NEW YORK.
LET'S FACE IT! BRAINS, BEAUTY— I HAD IT ALL!
UNTIL MY STUPID PARENTS SPLIT UP AND I WAS SENT INTO EXILE.
THAT'S NOT TRUE! YOU'RE BEING UNFAIR.

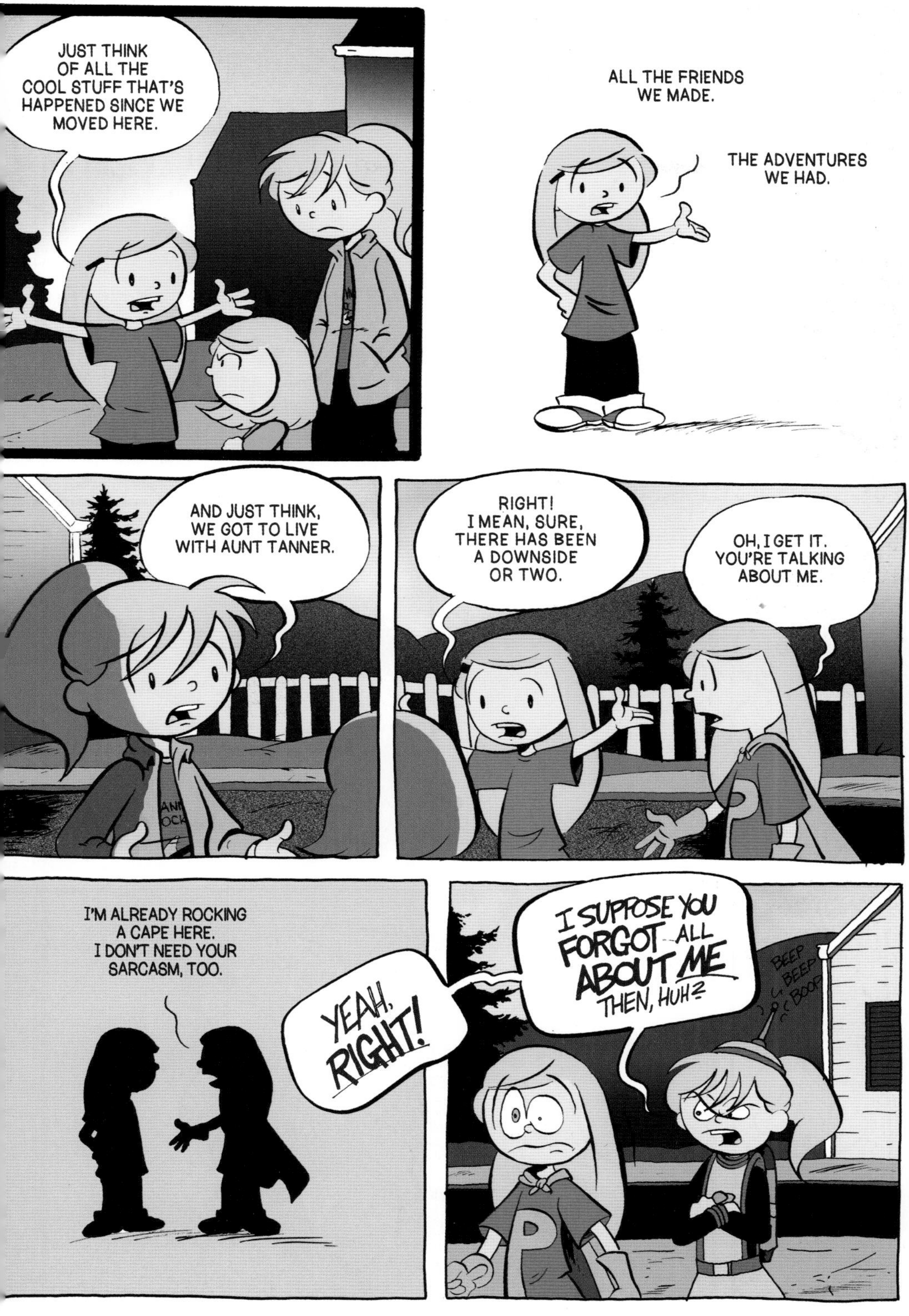

JUST THINK OF ALL THE COOL STUFF THAT'S HAPPENED SINCE WE MOVED HERE.
ALL THE FRIENDS WE MADE.
THE ADVENTURES WE HAD.
AND JUST THINK, WE GOT TO LIVE WITH AUNT TANNER.
RIGHT! I MEAN, SURE, THERE HAS BEEN A DOWNSIDE OR TWO.
OH, I GET IT. YOU'RE TALKING ABOUT ME.
I'M ALREADY ROCKING A CAPE HERE. I DON'T NEED YOUR SARCASM, TOO.
YEAH, RIGHT!
I SUPPOSE YOU FORGOT ALL ABOUT ME THEN, HUH?
BEEP BEEP BOOP

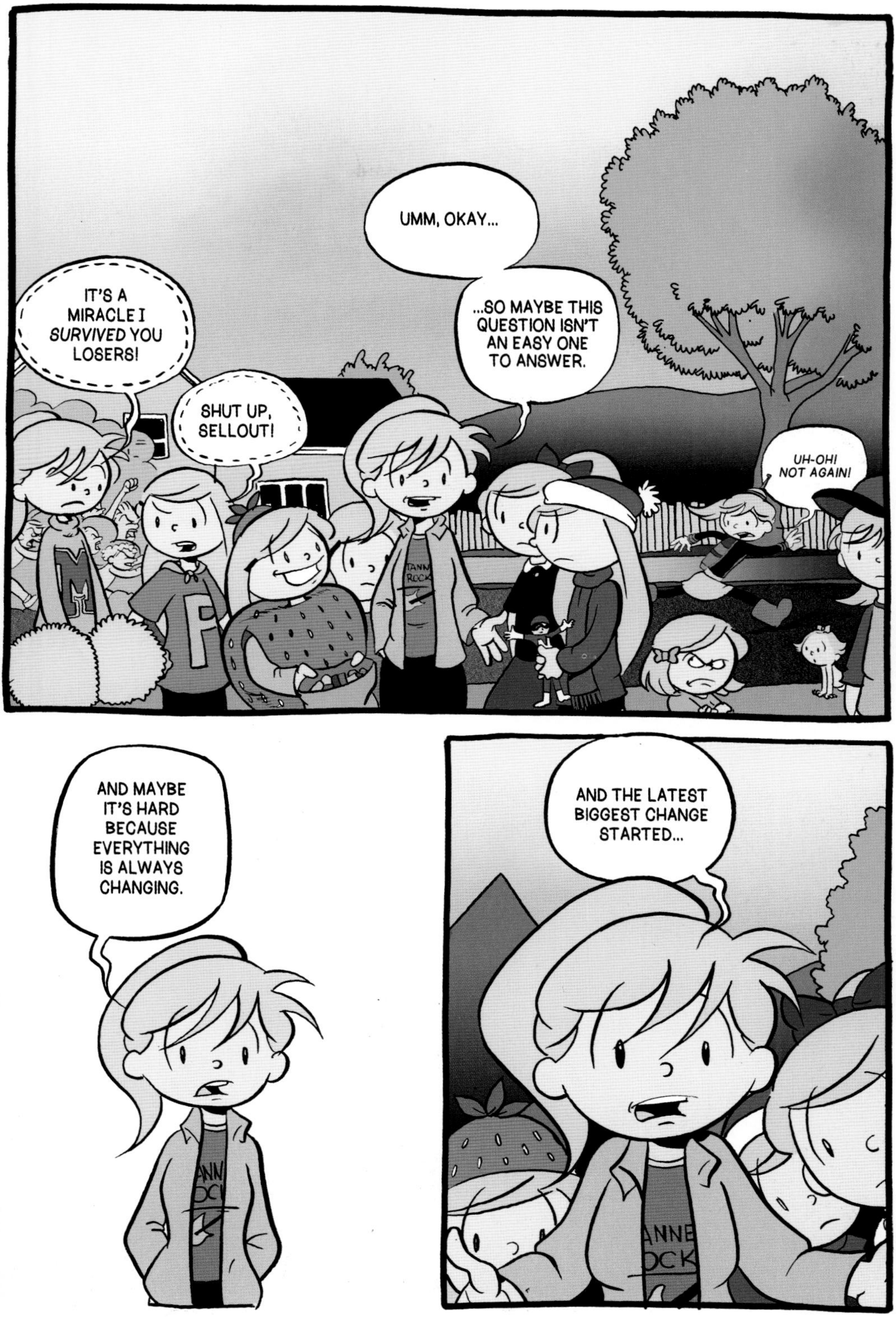
IT'S A MIRACLE I *SURVIVED* YOU LOSERS!
SHUT UP, SELLOUT!
UMM, OKAY...
...SO MAYBE THIS QUESTION ISN'T AN EASY ONE TO ANSWER.
UH-OH! NOT AGAIN!
AND MAYBE IT'S HARD BECAUSE EVERYTHING IS ALWAYS CHANGING.
AND THE LATEST BIGGEST CHANGE STARTED...

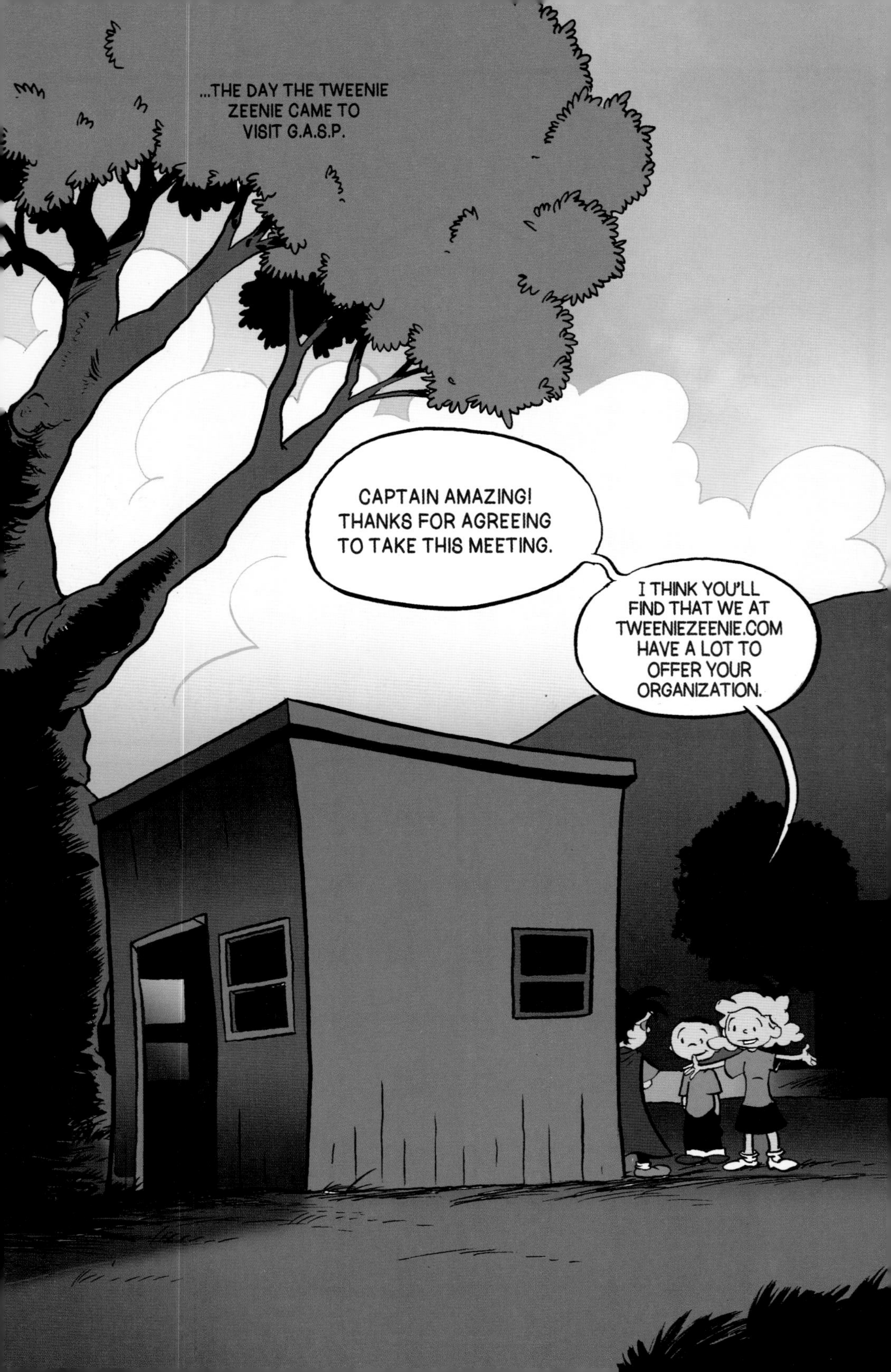
...THE DAY THE TWEENIE ZEENIE CAME TO VISIT G.A.S.P.
CAPTAIN AMAZING! THANKS FOR AGREEING TO TAKE THIS MEETING.
I THINK YOU'LL FIND THAT WE AT TWEENIEZEENIE.COM HAVE A LOT TO OFFER YOUR ORGANIZATION.

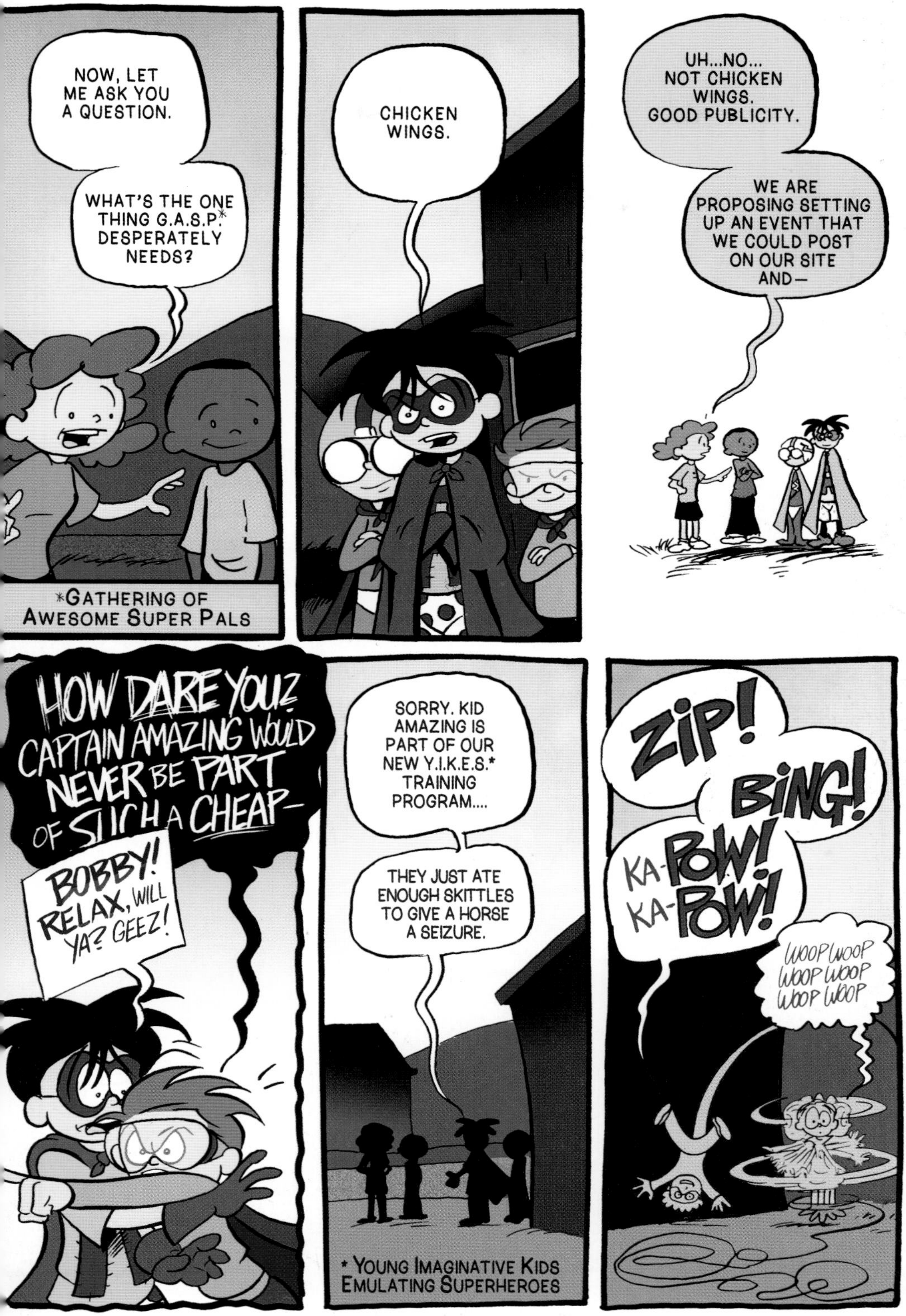
NOW, LET ME ASK YOU A QUESTION.
WHAT'S THE ONE THING G.A.S.P.* DESPERATELY NEEDS?
*GATHERING OF AWESOME SUPER PALS
CHICKEN WINGS.
UH...NO... NOT CHICKEN WINGS. GOOD PUBLICITY.
WE ARE PROPOSING SETTING UP AN EVENT THAT WE COULD POST ON OUR SITE AND—
HOW DARE YOU? CAPTAIN AMAZING WOULD NEVER BE PART OF SUCH A CHEAP—
BOBBY! RELAX, WILL YA? GEEZ!
SORRY. KID AMAZING IS PART OF OUR NEW Y.I.K.E.S.* TRAINING PROGRAM....
THEY JUST ATE ENOUGH SKITTLES TO GIVE A HORSE A SEIZURE.
* YOUNG IMAGINATIVE KIDS EMULATING SUPERHEROES
ZIP!
BING!
KA-POW! KA-POW!
WOOP WOOP WOOP WOOP WOOP WOOP

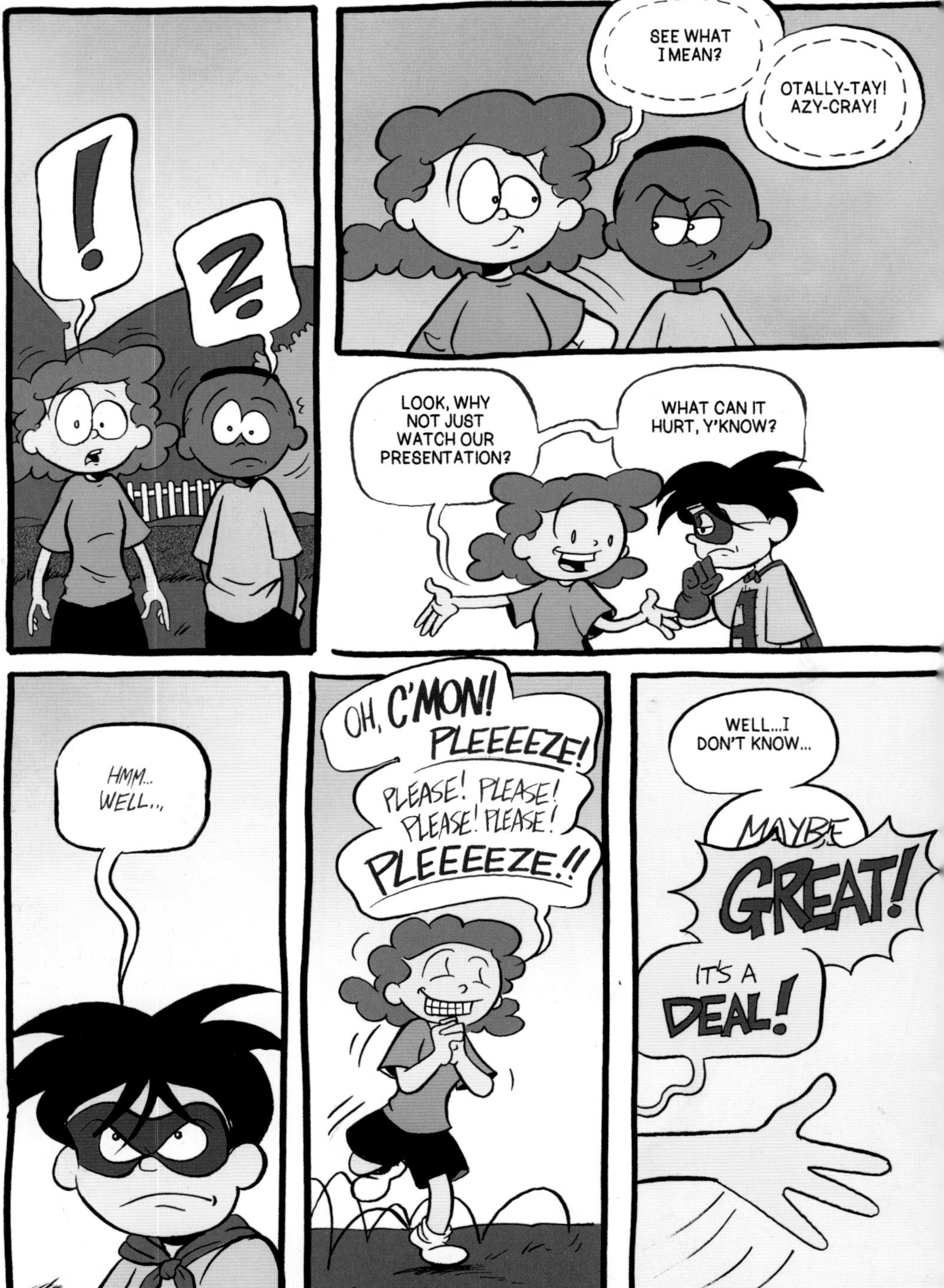
!
?
SEE WHAT I MEAN?
OTALLY-TAY! AZY-CRAY!
LOOK, WHY NOT JUST WATCH OUR PRESENTATION?
WHAT CAN IT HURT, Y'KNOW?
HMM... WELL...
OH, C'MON! PLEEEEZE!
PLEASE! PLEASE! PLEASE! PLEASE! PLEEEEZE!!
WELL...I DON'T KNOW...
MAYBE
GREAT!
IT'S A DEAL!

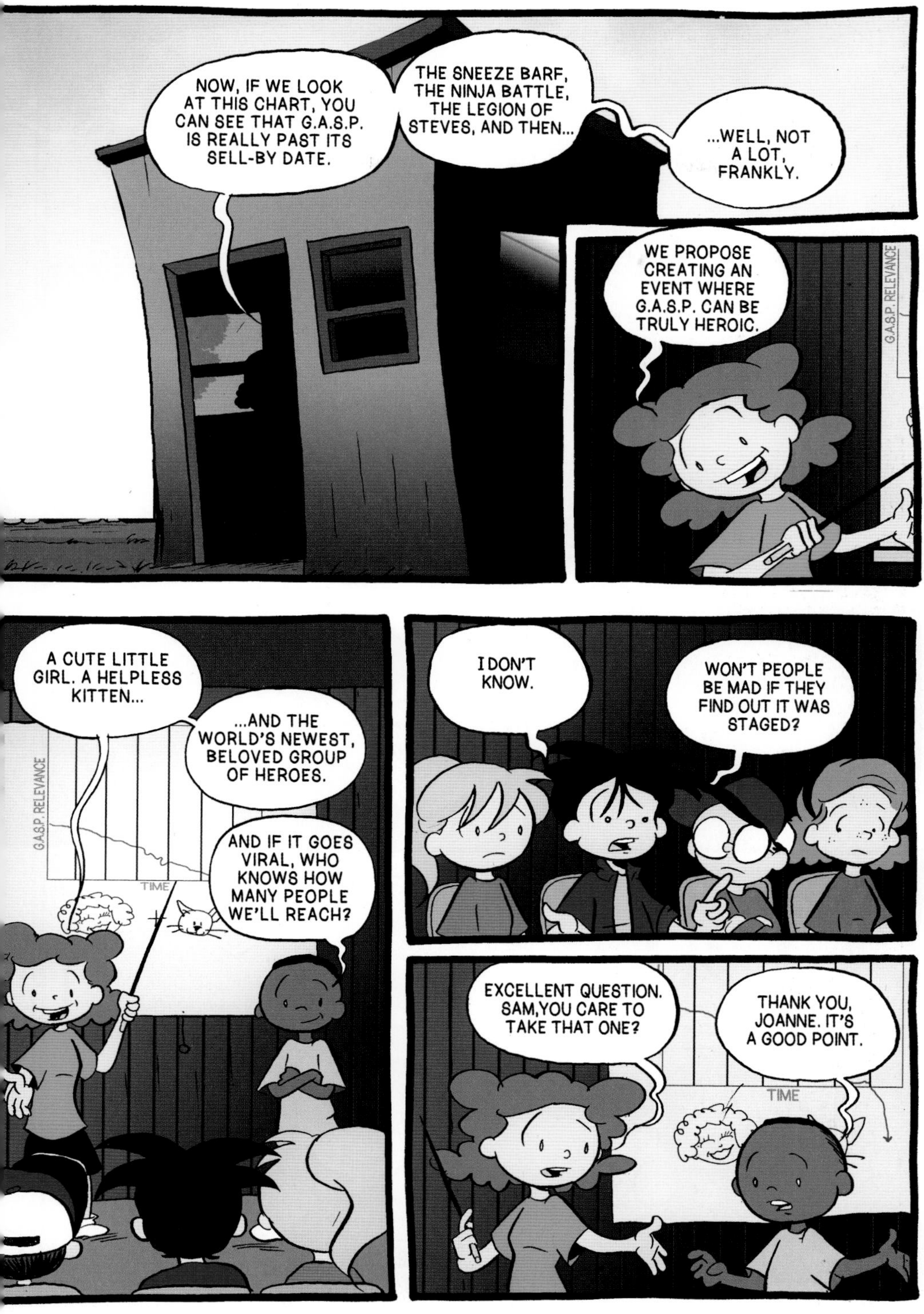

NOW, IF WE LOOK AT THIS CHART, YOU CAN SEE THAT G.A.S.P. IS REALLY PAST ITS SELL-BY DATE.
THE SNEEZE BARF, THE NINJA BATTLE, THE LEGION OF STEVES, AND THEN...
...WELL, NOT A LOT, FRANKLY.
WE PROPOSE CREATING AN EVENT WHERE G.A.S.P. CAN BE TRULY HEROIC.
G.A.S.P. RELEVANCE
A CUTE LITTLE GIRL. A HELPLESS KITTEN...
...AND THE WORLD'S NEWEST, BELOVED GROUP OF HEROES.
G.A.S.P. RELEVANCE
TIME
AND IF IT GOES VIRAL, WHO KNOWS HOW MANY PEOPLE WE'LL REACH?
I DON'T KNOW.
WON'T PEOPLE BE MAD IF THEY FIND OUT IT WAS STAGED?
EXCELLENT QUESTION. SAM,YOU CARE TO TAKE THAT ONE?
THANK YOU, JOANNE. IT'S A GOOD POINT.
TIME

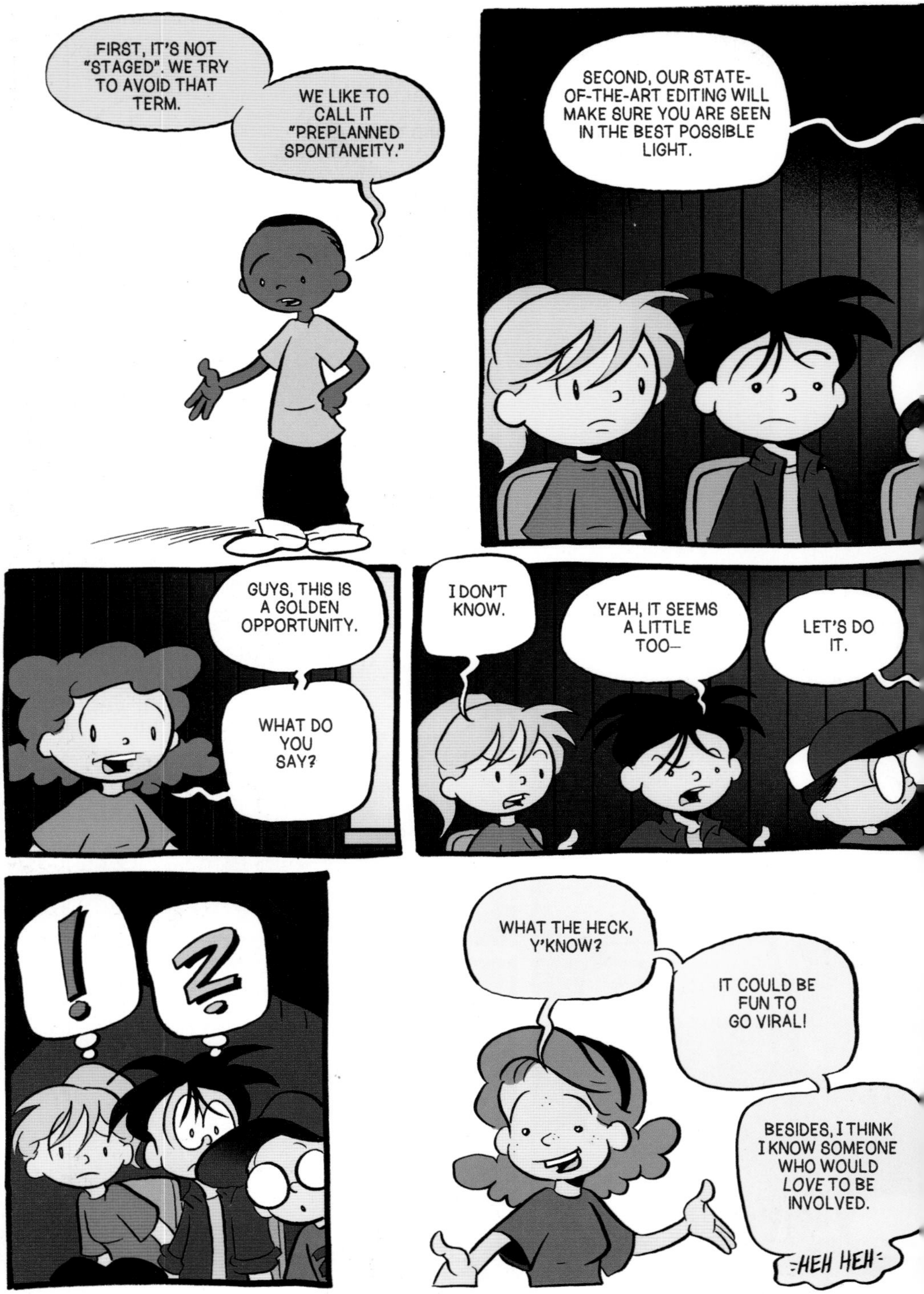
FIRST, IT'S NOT "STAGED". WE TRY TO AVOID THAT TERM.
WE LIKE TO CALL IT "PREPLANNED SPONTANEITY."
SECOND, OUR STATE-OF-THE-ART EDITING WILL MAKE SURE YOU ARE SEEN IN THE BEST POSSIBLE LIGHT.
GUYS, THIS IS A GOLDEN OPPORTUNITY.
WHAT DO YOU SAY?
I DON'T KNOW.
YEAH, IT SEEMS A LITTLE TOO—
LET'S DO IT.
!
?
WHAT THE HECK, Y'KNOW?
IT COULD BE FUN TO GO VIRAL!
BESIDES, I THINK I KNOW SOMEONE WHO WOULD *LOVE* TO BE INVOLVED.
HEH HEH

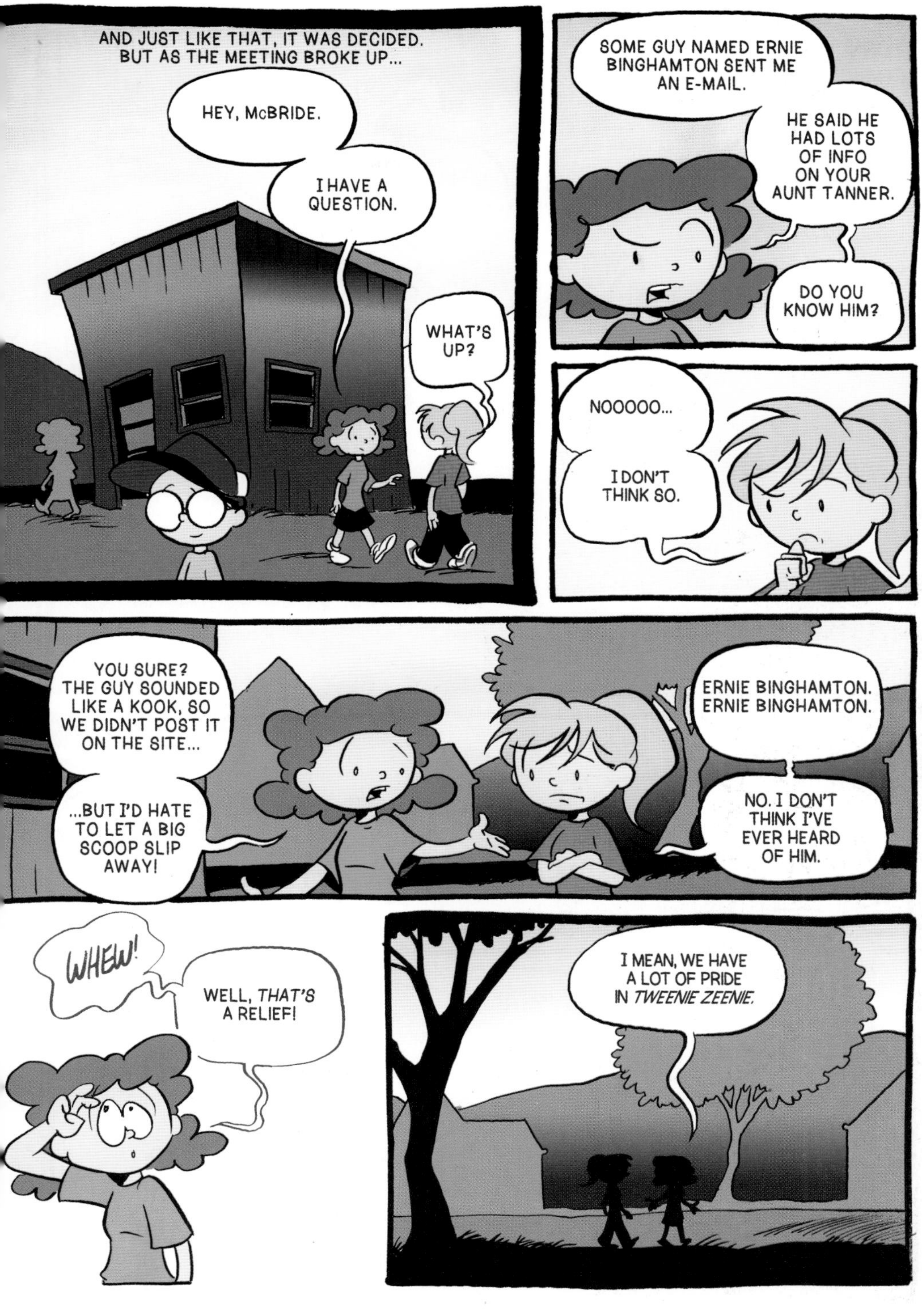
AND JUST LIKE THAT, IT WAS DECIDED. BUT AS THE MEETING BROKE UP...
HEY, McBRIDE.
I HAVE A QUESTION.
WHAT'S UP?
SOME GUY NAMED ERNIE BINGHAMTON SENT ME AN E-MAIL.
HE SAID HE HAD LOTS OF INFO ON YOUR AUNT TANNER.
DO YOU KNOW HIM?
NOOOOO...
I DON'T THINK SO.
YOU SURE? THE GUY SOUNDED LIKE A KOOK, SO WE DIDN'T POST IT ON THE SITE...
...BUT I'D HATE TO LET A BIG SCOOP SLIP AWAY!
ERNIE BINGHAMTON. ERNIE BINGHAMTON.
NO. I DON'T THINK I'VE EVER HEARD OF HIM.
WHEW!
WELL, *THAT'S* A RELIEF!
I MEAN, WE HAVE A LOT OF PRIDE IN *TWEENIE ZEENIE.*

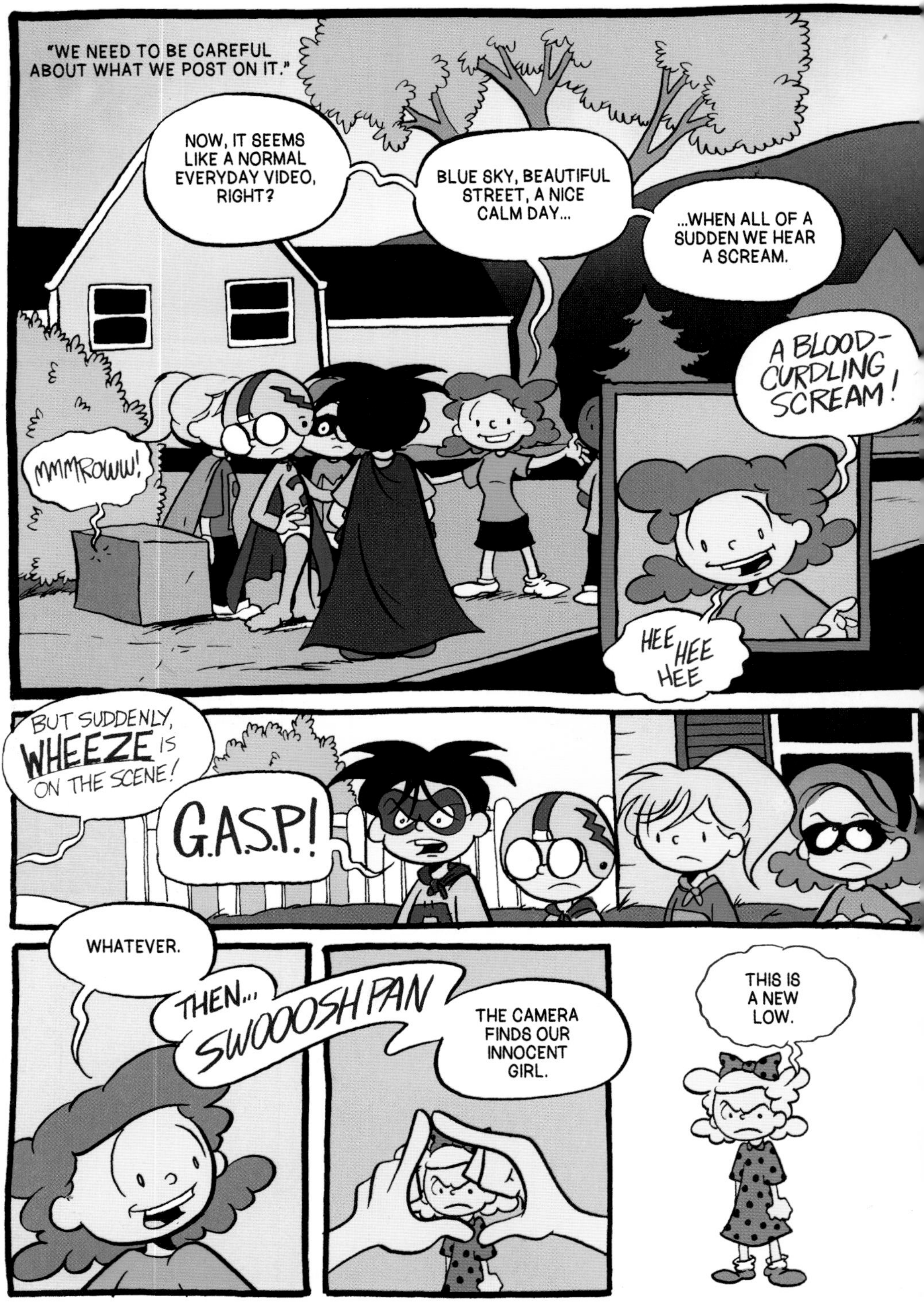
"WE NEED TO BE CAREFUL ABOUT WHAT WE POST ON IT."
NOW, IT SEEMS LIKE A NORMAL EVERYDAY VIDEO, RIGHT?
BLUE SKY, BEAUTIFUL STREET, A NICE CALM DAY...
...WHEN ALL OF A SUDDEN WE HEAR A SCREAM.
MMMROWW!
A BLOOD-CURDLING SCREAM!
HEE HEE HEE
BUT SUDDENLY, WHEEZE IS ON THE SCENE!
G.A.S.P.!
WHATEVER.
THEN... SWOOOSH PAN
THE CAMERA FINDS OUR INNOCENT GIRL.
THIS IS A NEW LOW.

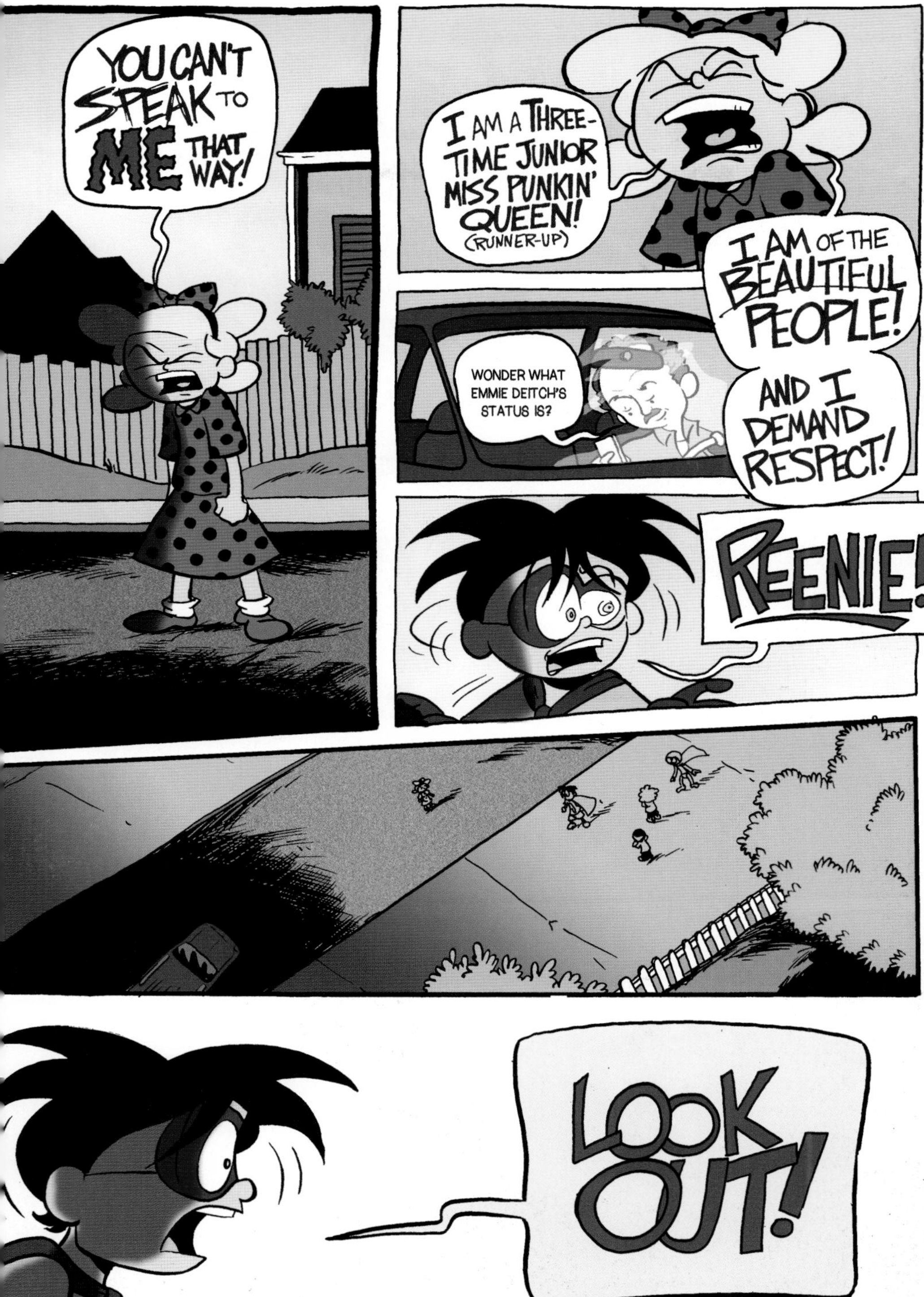
YOU CAN'T SPEAK TO ME THAT WAY!
I AM A THREE-TIME JUNIOR MISS PUNKIN' QUEEN! (RUNNER-UP)
I AM OF THE BEAUTIFUL PEOPLE!
WONDER WHAT EMMIE DEITCH'S STATUS IS?
AND I DEMAND RESPECT!
REENIE!
LOOK OUT!

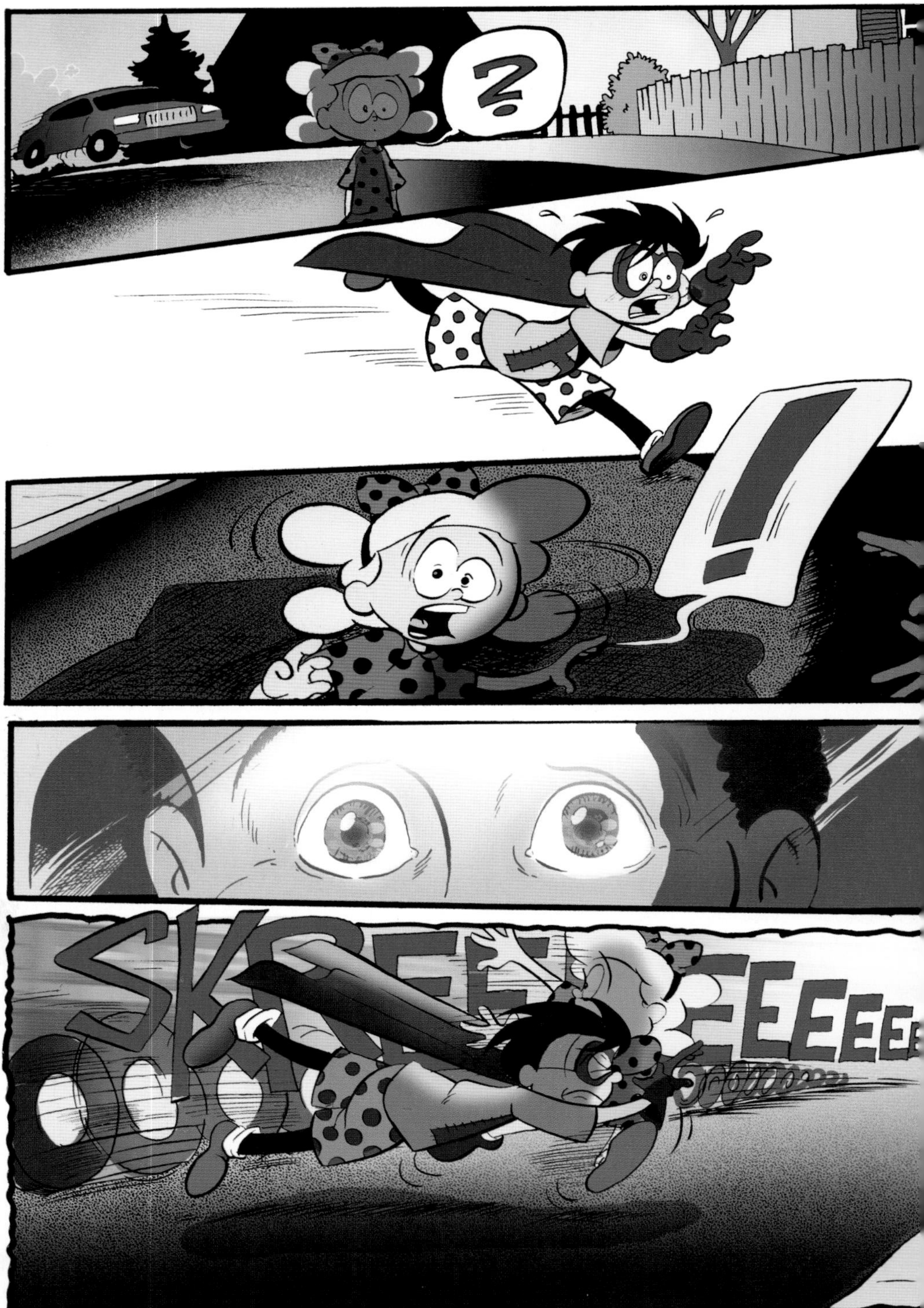
?
!

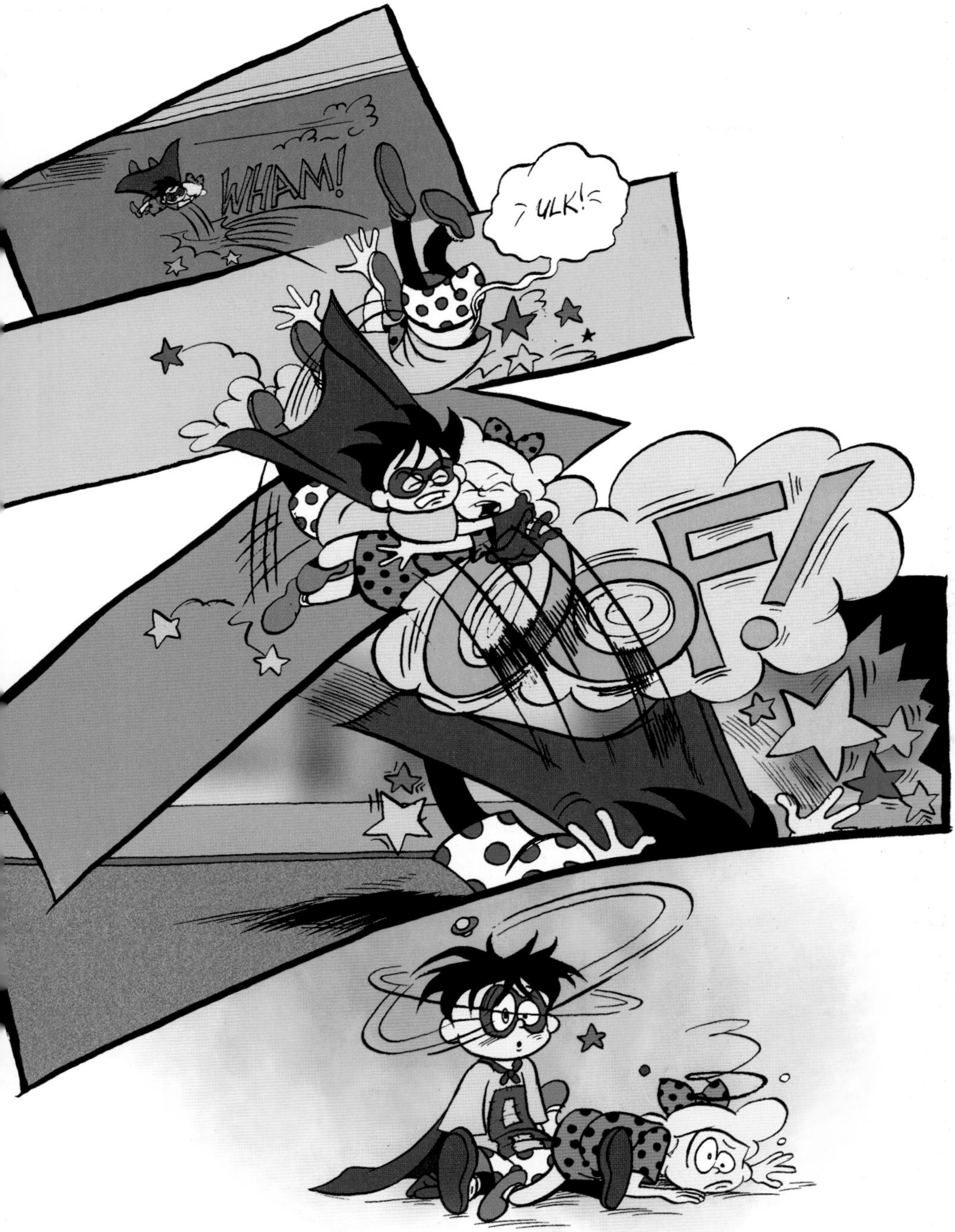
WHAM!
ULK!
F!

JACKPOT.

AND SHE WAS RIGHT!

ONCE HANNIGAN POSTED THE VIDEO ON TWEENIEZEENIE.COM, IT BECAME A SENSATION!

IN THE FIRST WEEK ALONE, THE VIDEO RECEIVED...

175,000 HITS!

WHICH, AFTER SOMEONE PHOTOSHOPPED IN SOME LIGHTSABERS, CLIMBED

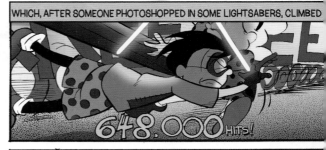

648,000 HITS!

AND FINALLY, ONCE HANNIGAN GOT HER KITTEN IN...

2,000,000 HITS!

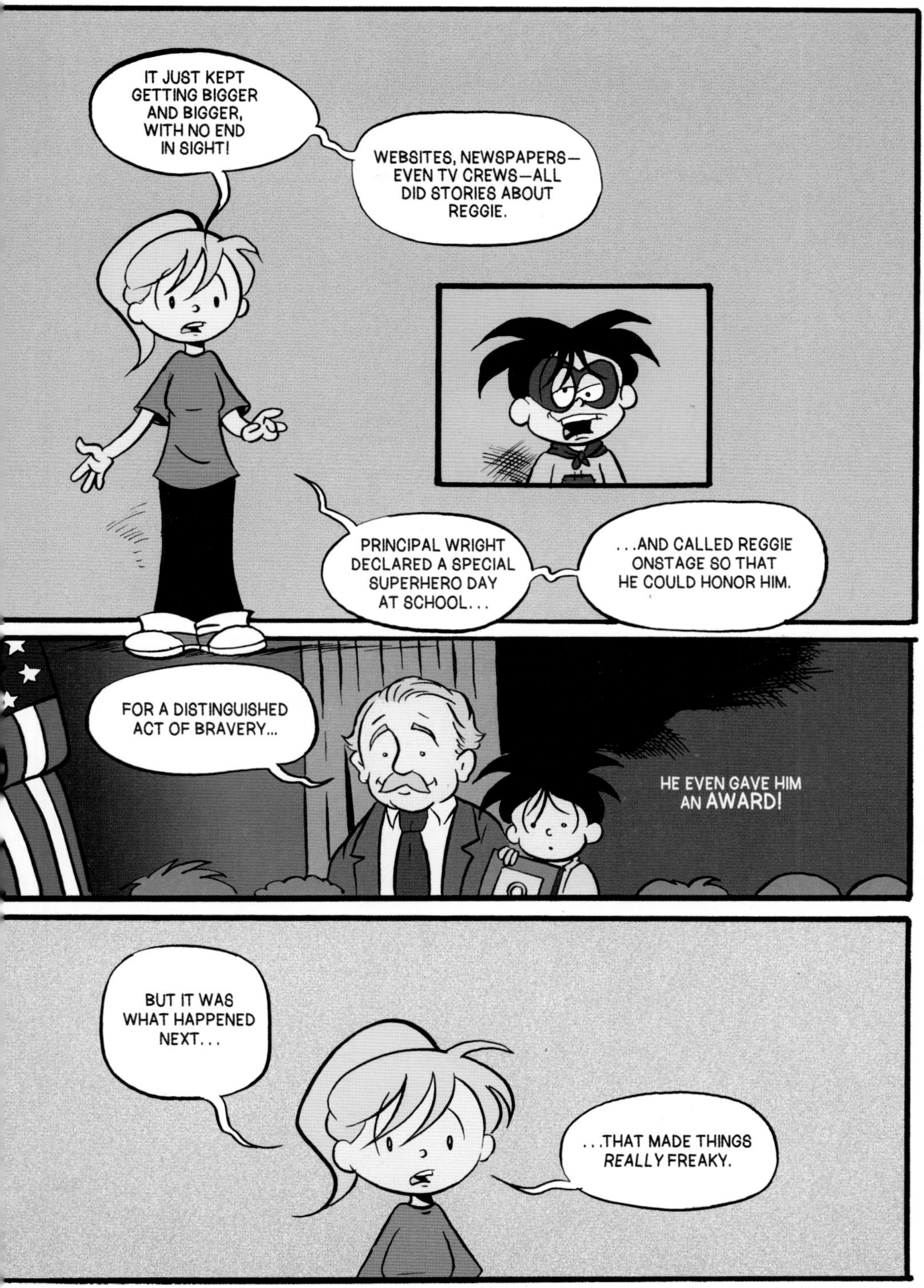
IT JUST KEPT GETTING BIGGER AND BIGGER, WITH NO END IN SIGHT!
WEBSITES, NEWSPAPERS—EVEN TV CREWS—ALL DID STORIES ABOUT REGGIE.
PRINCIPAL WRIGHT DECLARED A SPECIAL SUPERHERO DAY AT SCHOOL. . .
. . .AND CALLED REGGIE ONSTAGE SO THAT HE COULD HONOR HIM.
FOR A DISTINGUISHED ACT OF BRAVERY...
HE EVEN GAVE HIM AN AWARD!
BUT IT WAS WHAT HAPPENED NEXT. . .
. . .THAT MADE THINGS *REALLY* FREAKY.

26

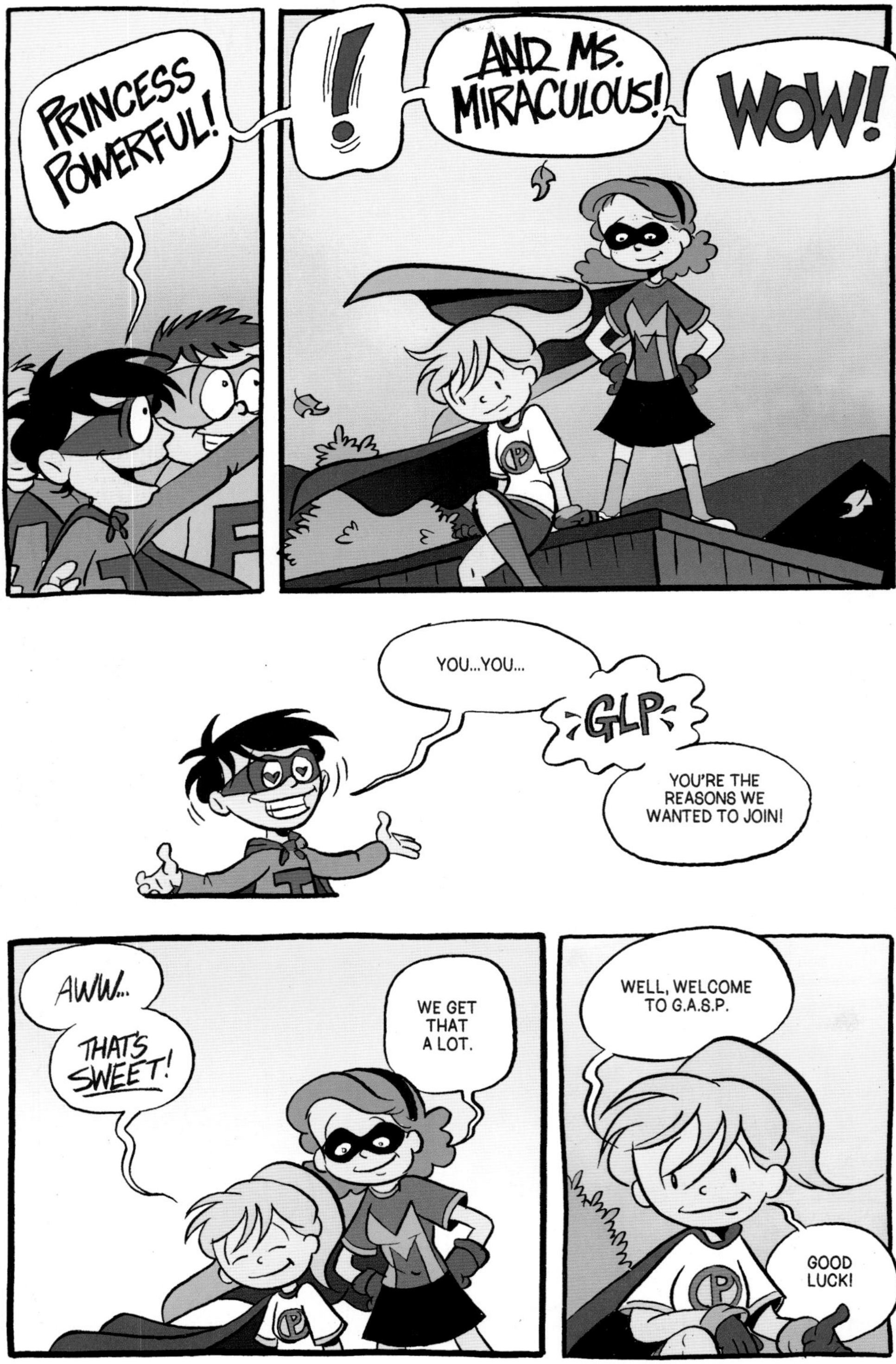
PRINCESS POWERFUL!
!
AND MS. MIRACULOUS!
WOW!
YOU...YOU...
GLP
YOU'RE THE REASONS WE WANTED TO JOIN!
AWW...
THAT'S SWEET!
WE GET THAT A LOT.
WELL, WELCOME TO G.A.S.P.
GOOD LUCK!

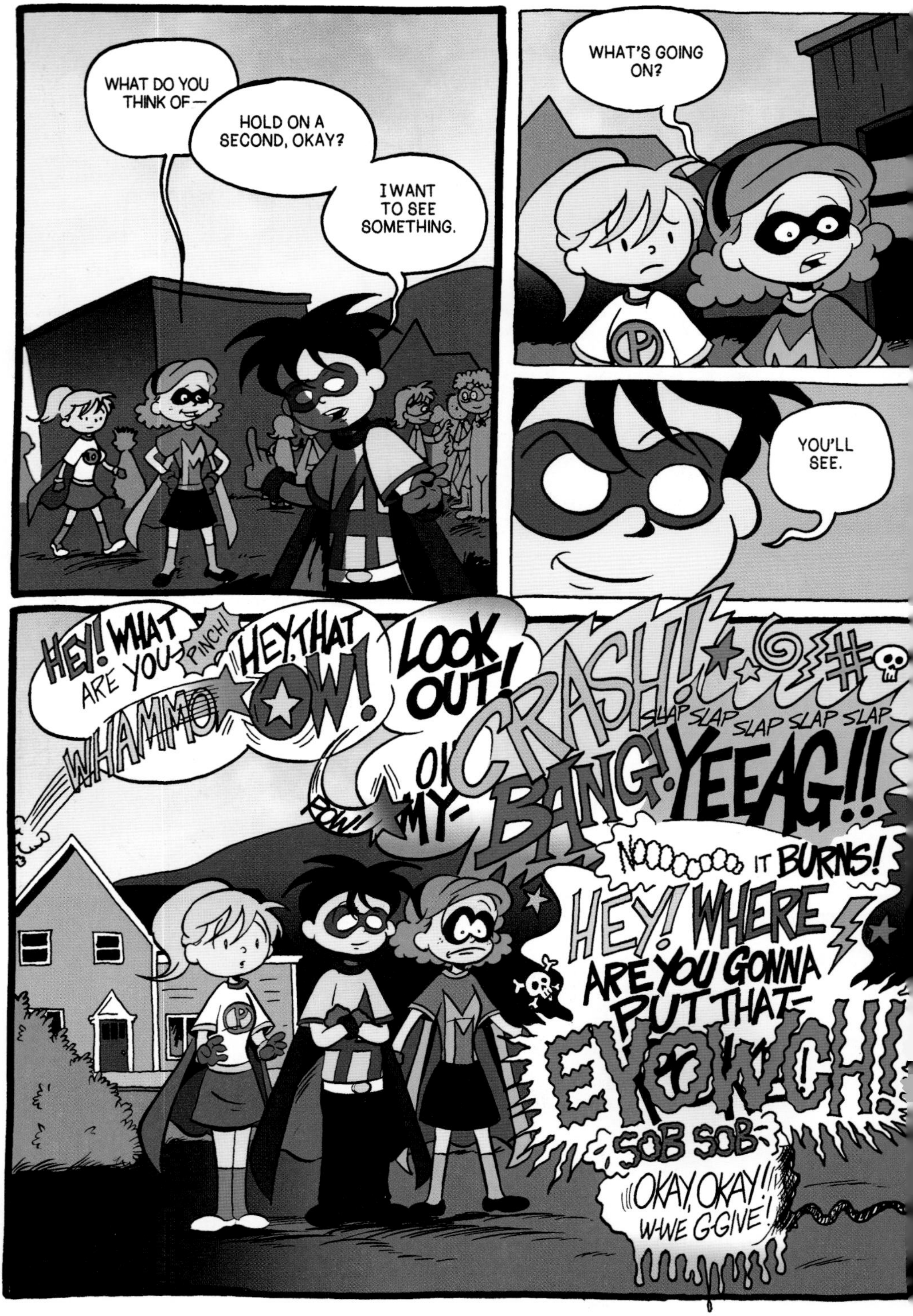
WHAT DO YOU THINK OF—
HOLD ON A SECOND, OKAY?
I WANT TO SEE SOMETHING.
WHAT'S GOING ON?
YOU'LL SEE.
HEY! WHAT ARE YOU-
PINCH!
HEY, THAT
OW!
WHAMMO
LOOK OUT!
CRASH!!
OI MY-
POW!
SLAP SLAP SLAP SLAP SLAP
BANG!
YEEAG!!
NOOOOOOOO IT BURNS!
HEY! WHERE ARE YOU GONNA PUT THAT-
EYOWCH!!
SOB SOB
OKAY, OKAY! W-WE G-GIVE!

34

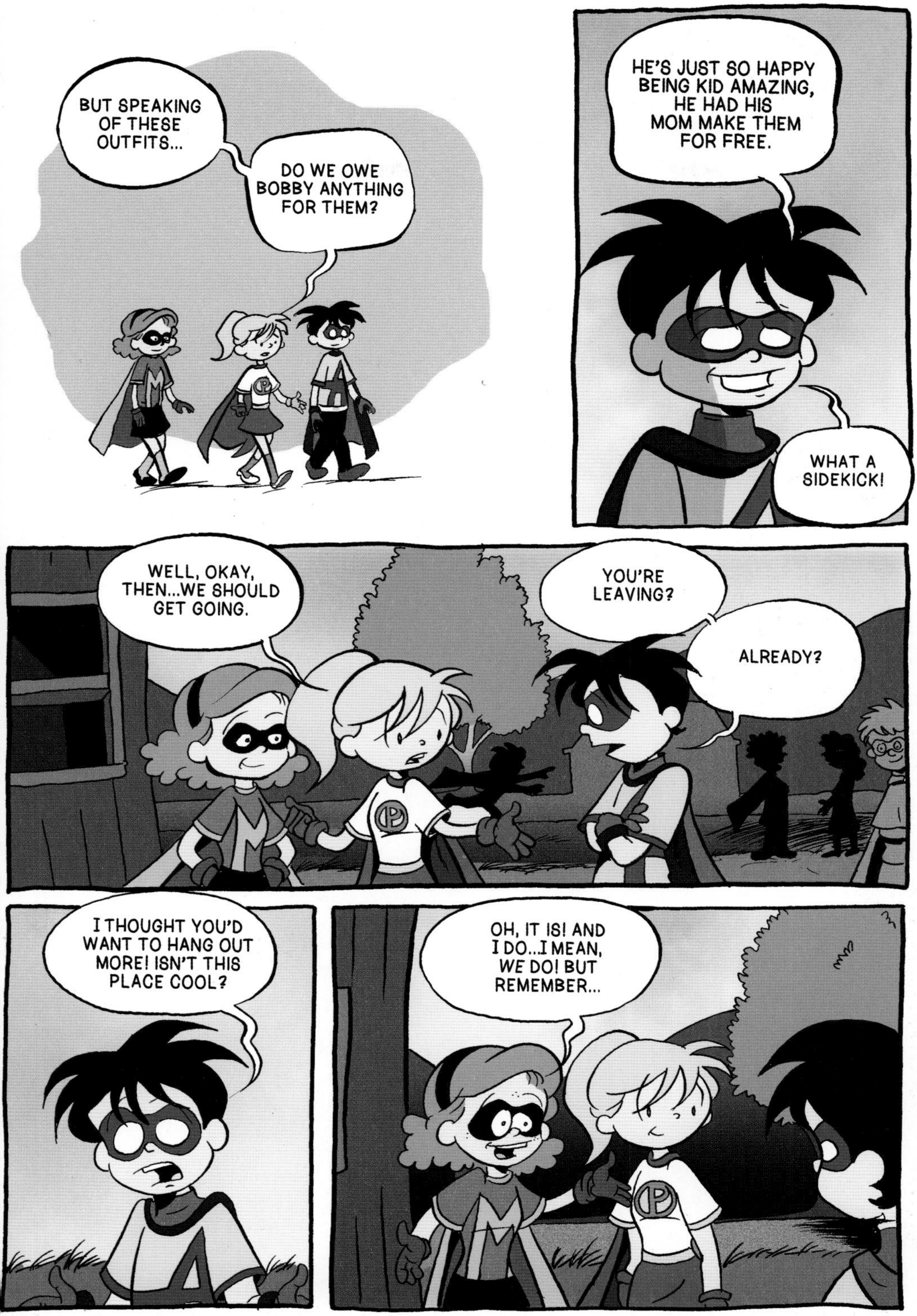
BUT SPEAKING OF THESE OUTFITS...
DO WE OWE BOBBY ANYTHING FOR THEM?
HE'S JUST SO HAPPY BEING KID AMAZING, HE HAD HIS MOM MAKE THEM FOR FREE.
WHAT A SIDEKICK!
WELL, OKAY, THEN...WE SHOULD GET GOING.
YOU'RE LEAVING?
ALREADY?
I THOUGHT YOU'D WANT TO HANG OUT MORE! ISN'T THIS PLACE COOL?
OH, IT IS! AND I DO...I MEAN, *WE* DO! BUT REMEMBER...

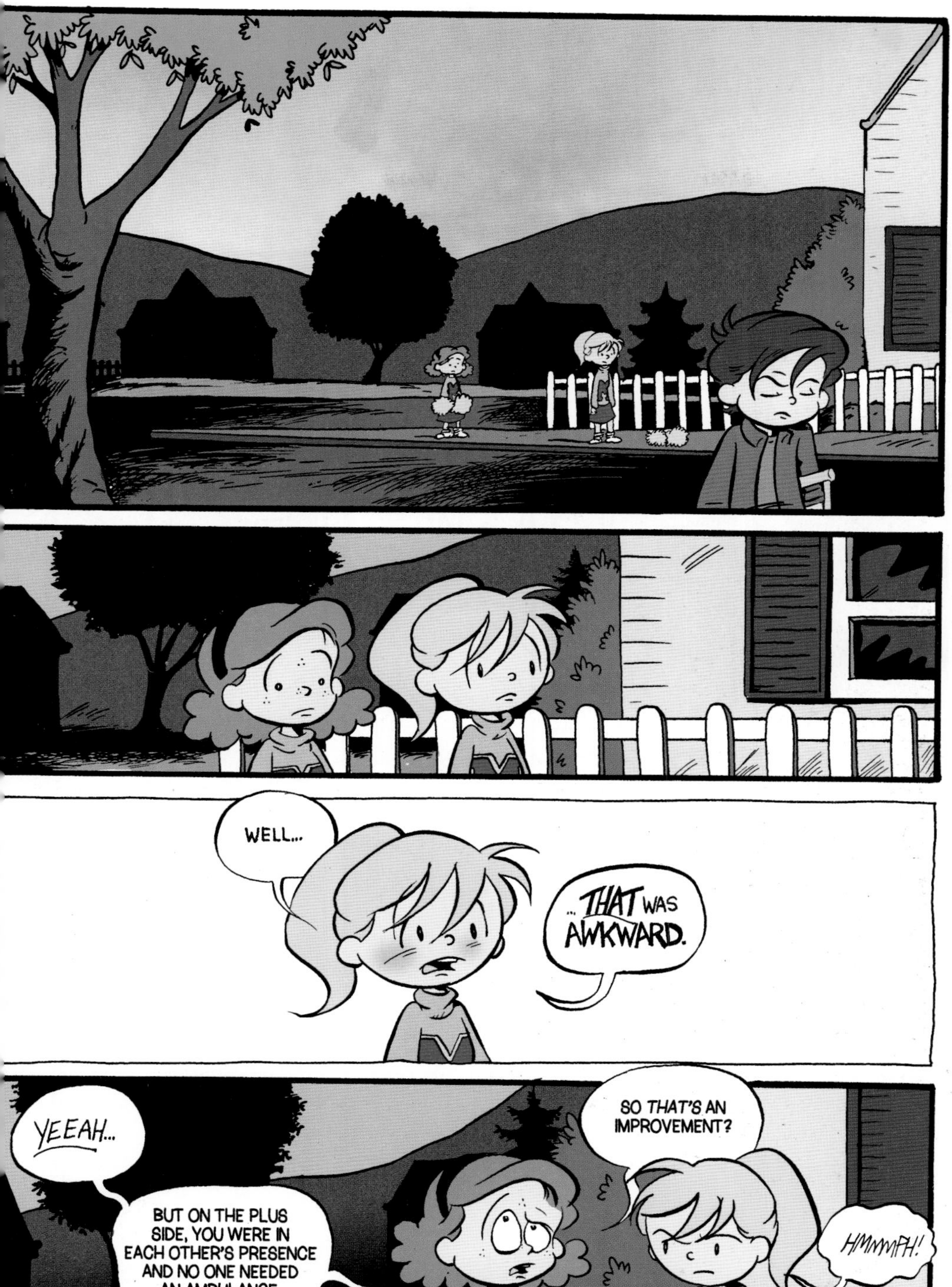
WELL...
...THAT WAS AWKWARD.
YEEAH...
BUT ON THE PLUS SIDE, YOU WERE IN EACH OTHER'S PRESENCE AND NO ONE NEEDED AN AMBULANCE.
SO THAT'S AN IMPROVEMENT?
HMMMPH!

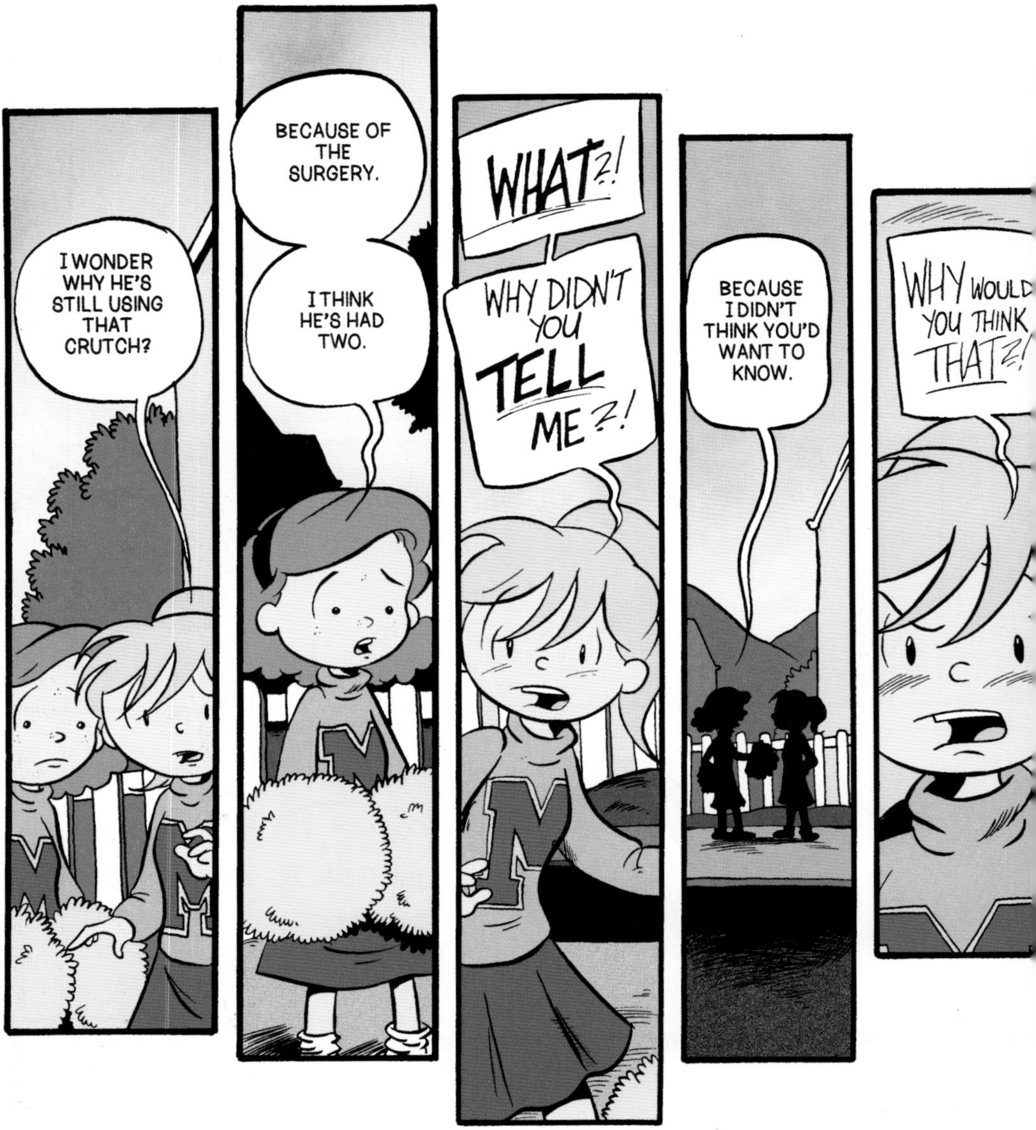
I WONDER WHY HE'S STILL USING THAT CRUTCH?
BECAUSE OF THE SURGERY.
I THINK HE'S HAD TWO.
WHAT?!
WHY DIDN'T YOU TELL ME?!
BECAUSE I DIDN'T THINK YOU'D WANT TO KNOW.
WHY WOULD YOU THINK THAT?!

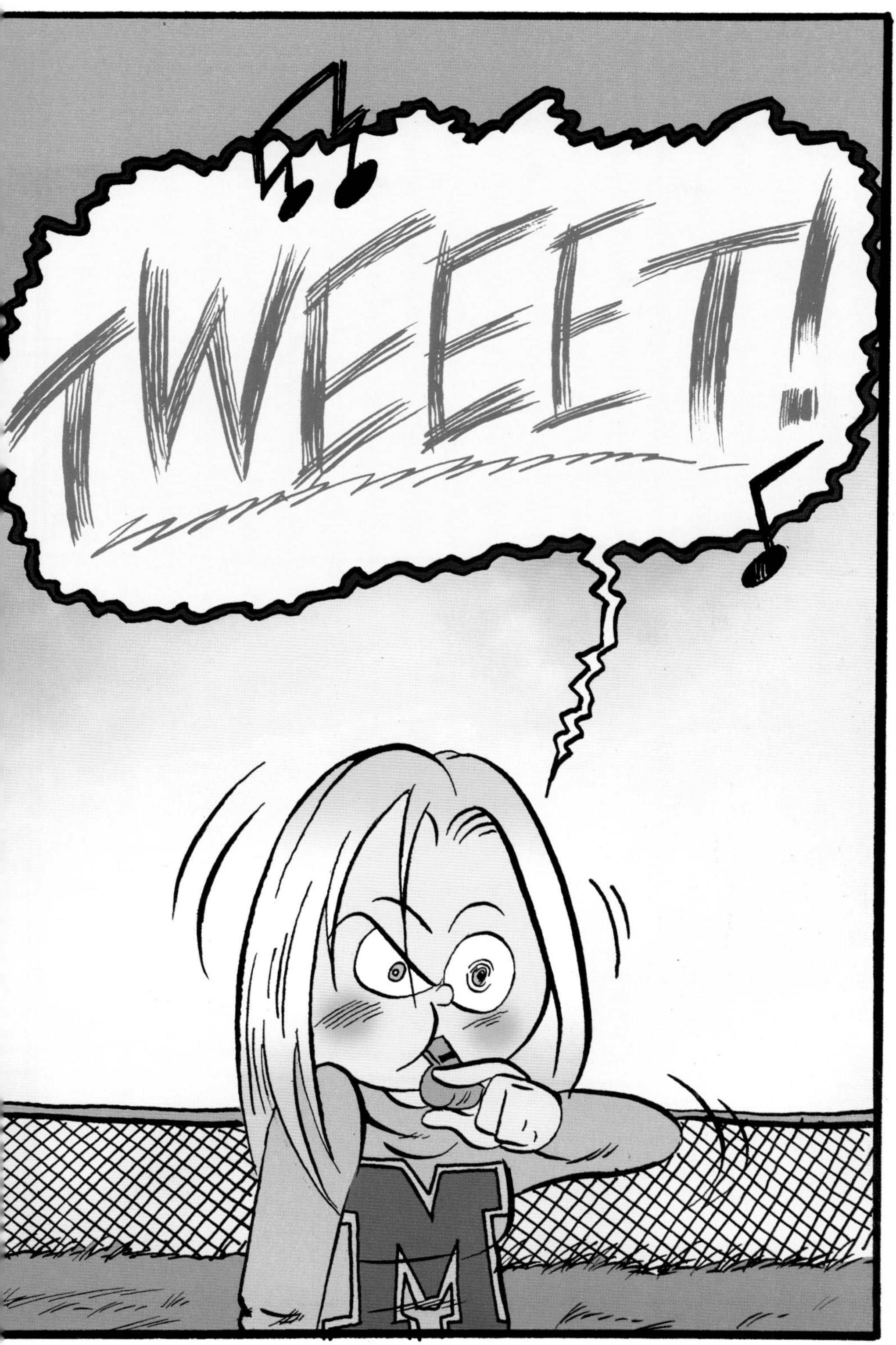
TWEEET!

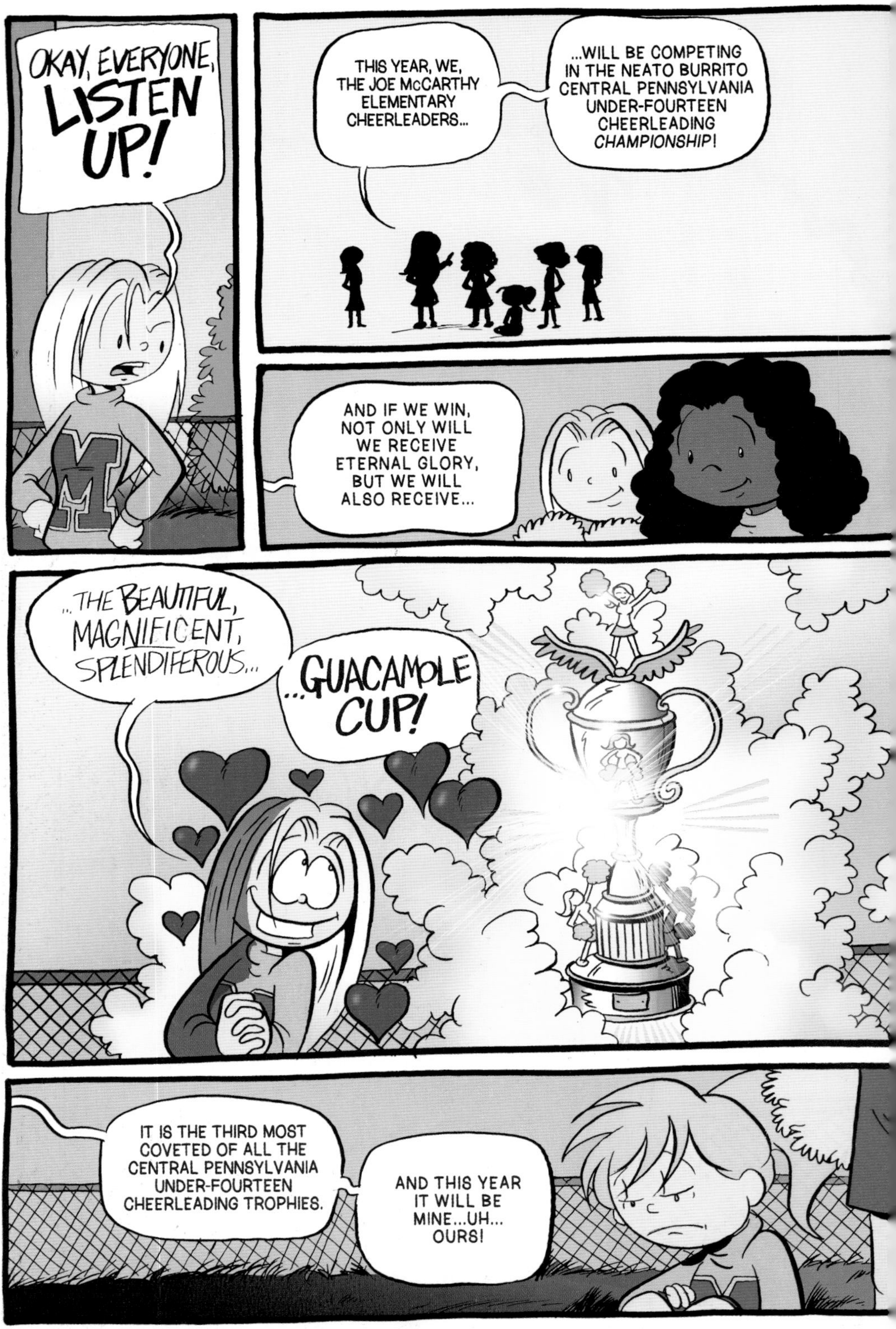
OKAY, EVERYONE, LISTEN UP!
THIS YEAR, WE, THE JOE McCARTHY ELEMENTARY CHEERLEADERS...
...WILL BE COMPETING IN THE NEATO BURRITO CENTRAL PENNSYLVANIA UNDER-FOURTEEN CHEERLEADING CHAMPIONSHIP!
AND IF WE WIN, NOT ONLY WILL WE RECEIVE ETERNAL GLORY, BUT WE WILL ALSO RECEIVE...
...THE BEAUTIFUL, MAGNIFICENT, SPLENDIFEROUS...
...GUACAMOLE CUP!
IT IS THE THIRD MOST COVETED OF ALL THE CENTRAL PENNSYLVANIA UNDER-FOURTEEN CHEERLEADING TROPHIES.
AND THIS YEAR IT WILL BE MINE...UH... OURS!

49

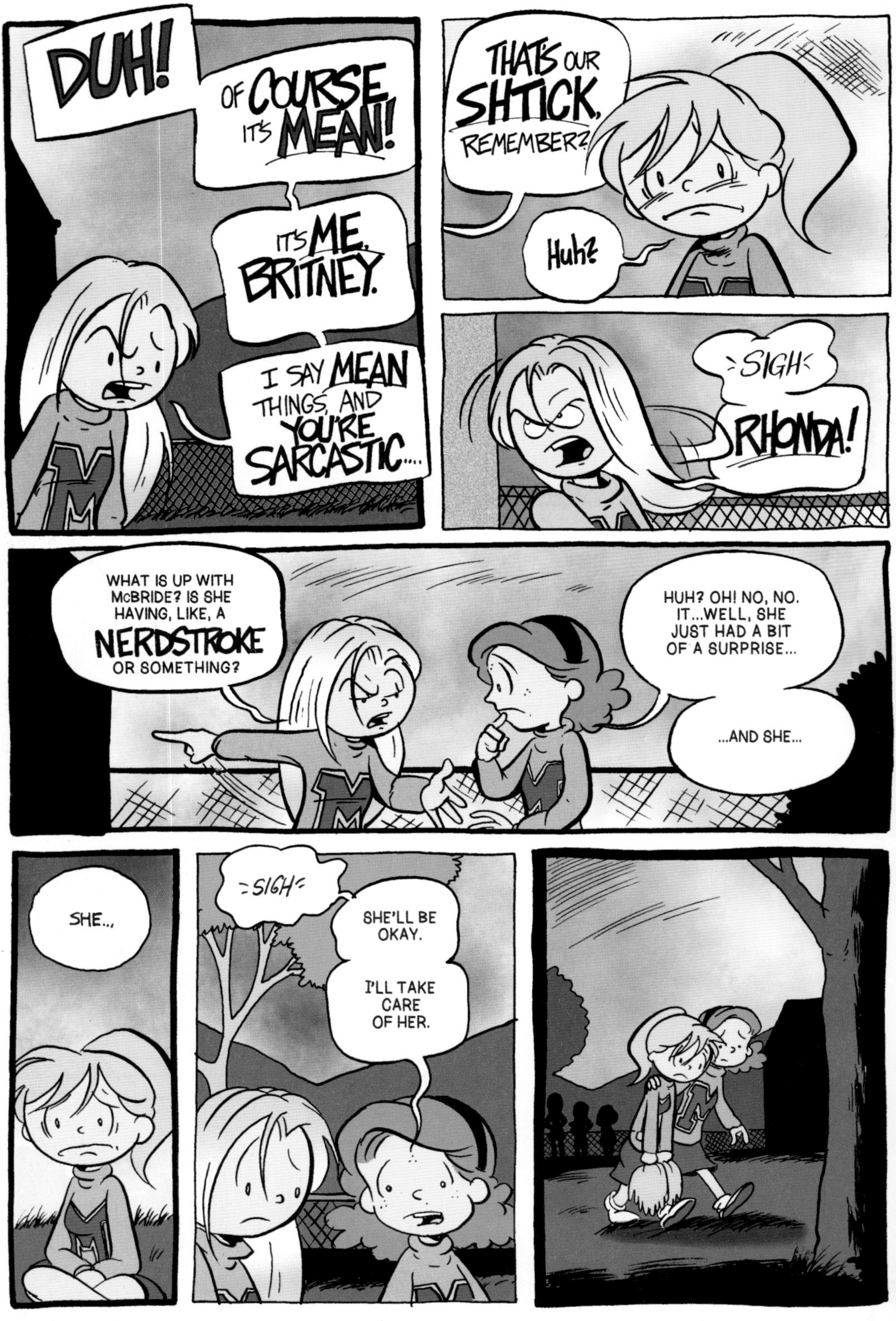
DUH!
OF COURSE IT'S MEAN!
IT'S ME, BRITNEY.
I SAY MEAN THINGS, AND YOU'RE SARCASTIC....
THAT'S OUR SHTICK, REMEMBER?
Huh?
SIGH
RHONDA!
WHAT IS UP WITH McBRIDE? IS SHE HAVING, LIKE, A NERDSTROKE OR SOMETHING?
HUH? OH! NO, NO. IT...WELL, SHE JUST HAD A BIT OF A SURPRISE...
...AND SHE...
SHE...
SIGH
SHE'LL BE OKAY.
I'LL TAKE CARE OF HER.

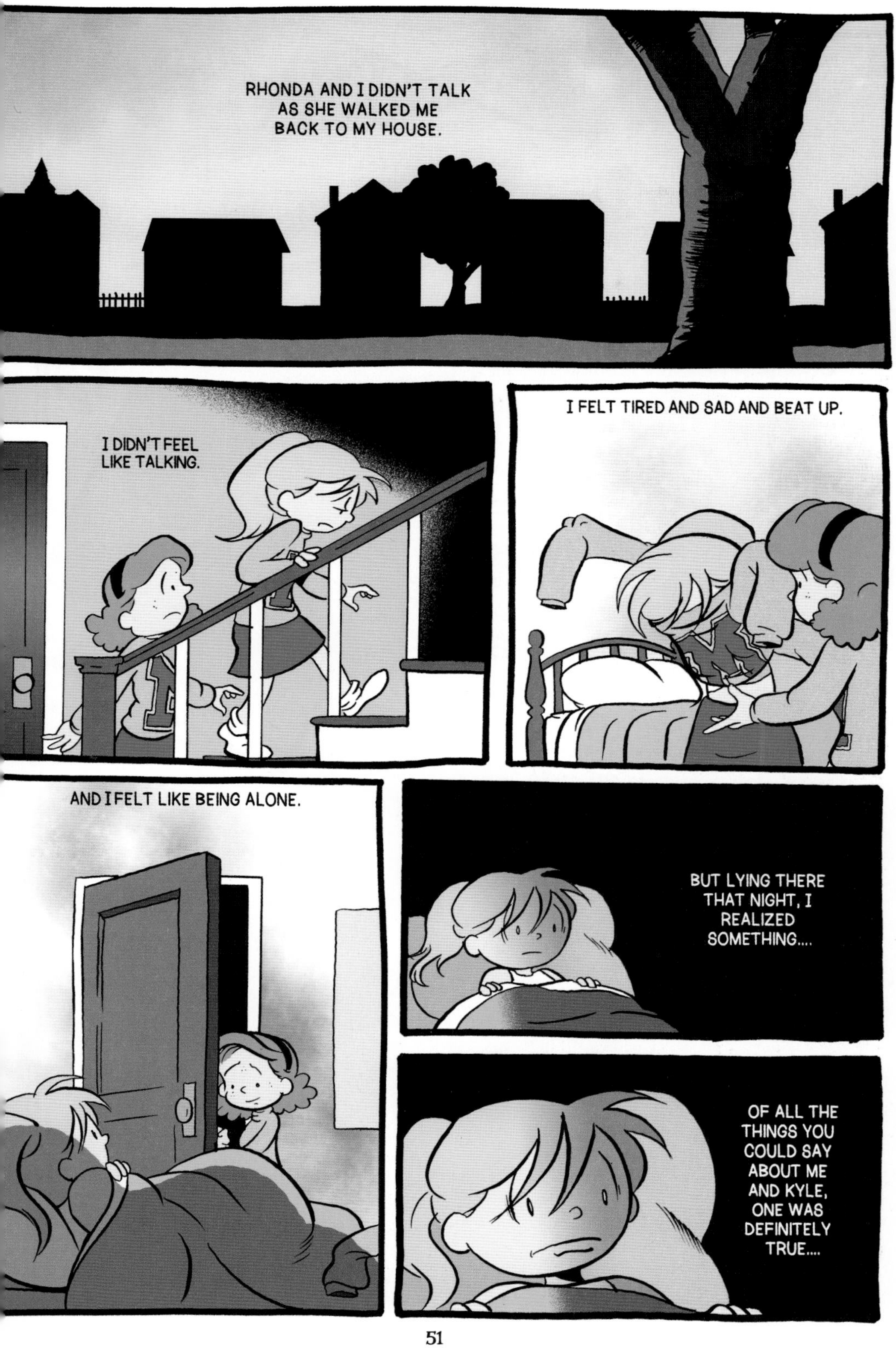
RHONDA AND I DIDN'T TALK AS SHE WALKED ME BACK TO MY HOUSE.
I DIDN'T FEEL LIKE TALKING.
I FELT TIRED AND SAD AND BEAT UP.
AND I FELT LIKE BEING ALONE.
BUT LYING THERE THAT NIGHT, I REALIZED SOMETHING....
OF ALL THE THINGS YOU COULD SAY ABOUT ME AND KYLE, ONE WAS DEFINITELY TRUE....

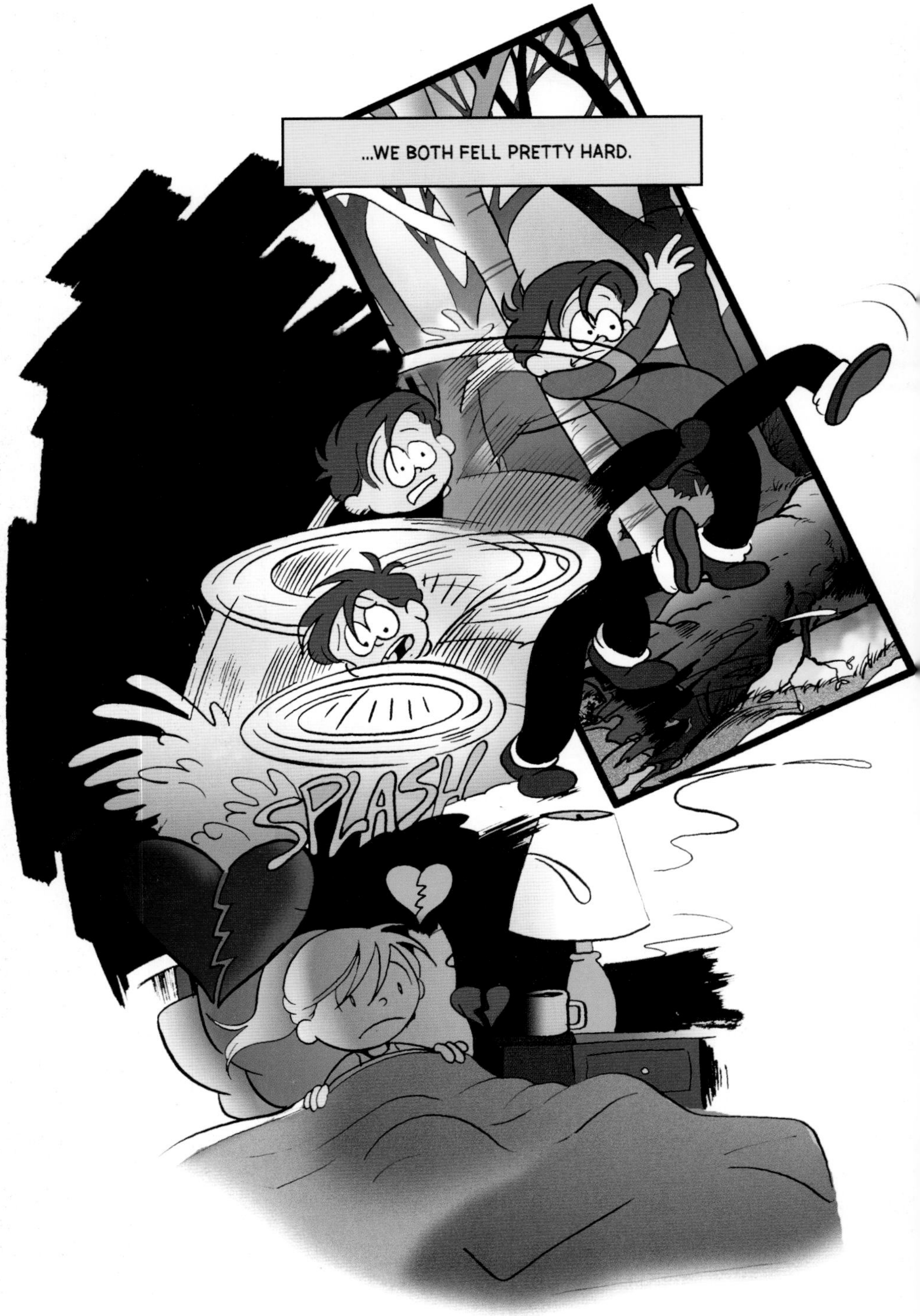
...WE BOTH FELL PRETTY HARD.
SPLASH

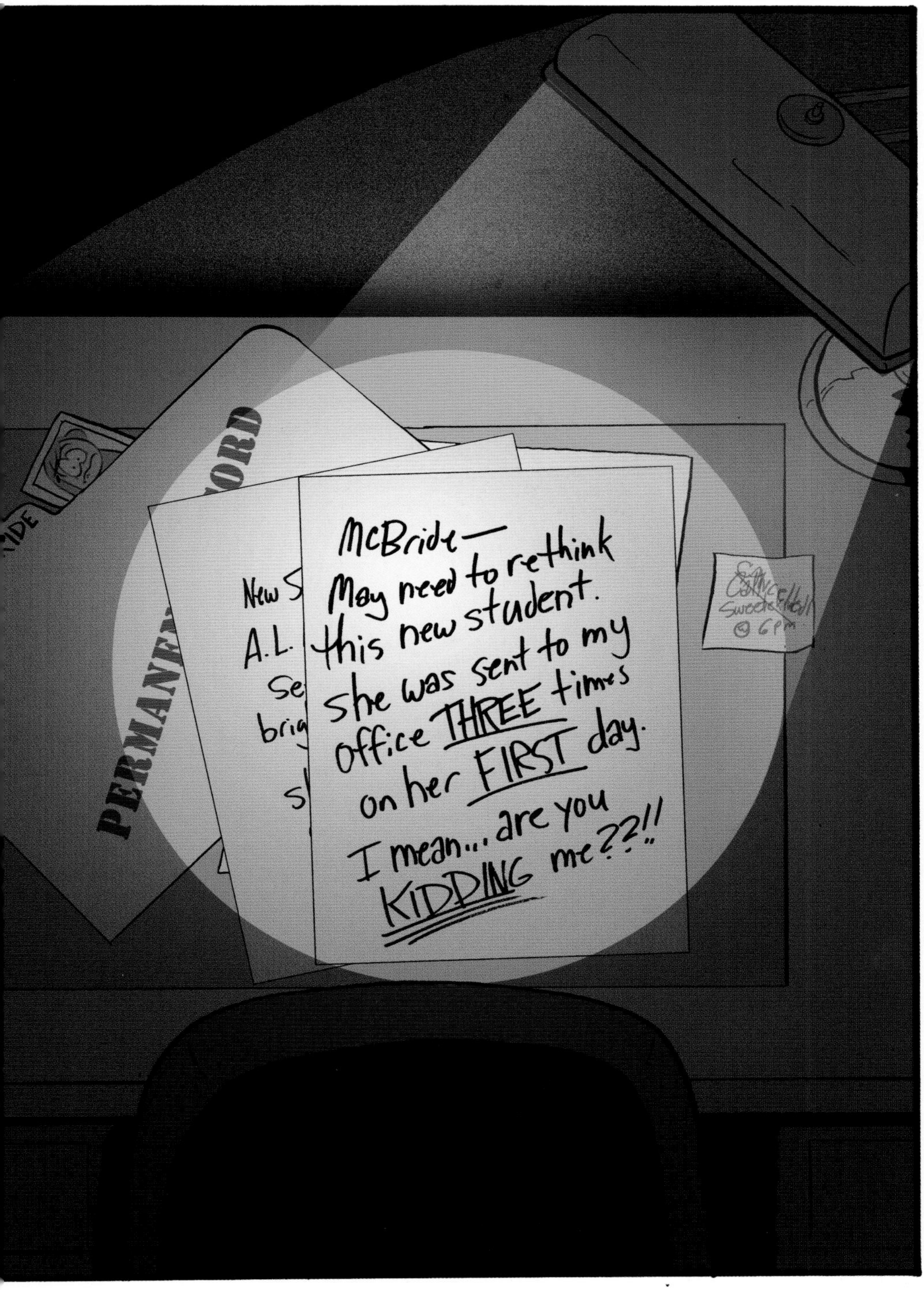
McBride—
May need to rethink
this new student.
she was sent to my
office THREE times
on her FIRST day.
I mean... are you
KIDDING me??!!

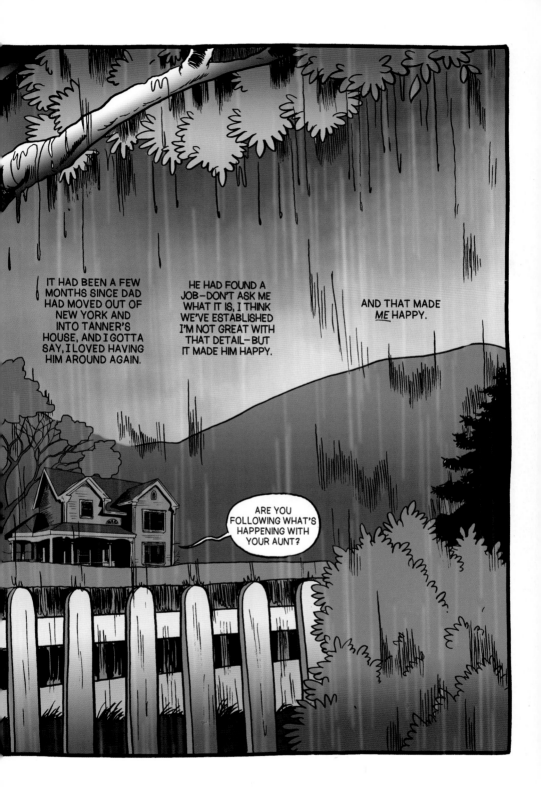

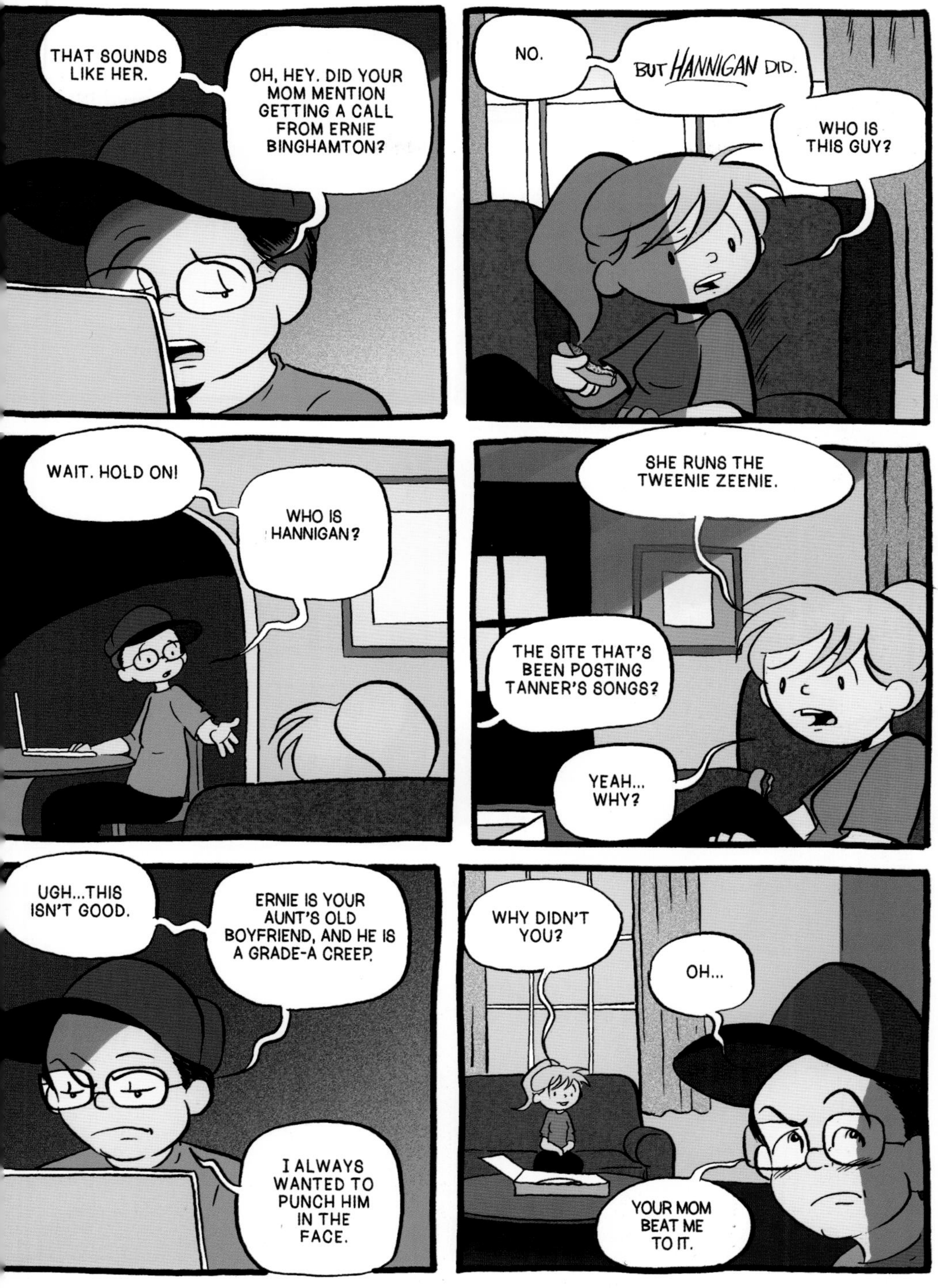
THAT SOUNDS LIKE HER.
OH, HEY. DID YOUR MOM MENTION GETTING A CALL FROM ERNIE BINGHAMTON?
NO.
BUT HANNIGAN DID.
WHO IS THIS GUY?
WAIT. HOLD ON!
WHO IS HANNIGAN?
SHE RUNS THE TWEENIE ZEENIE.
THE SITE THAT'S BEEN POSTING TANNER'S SONGS?
YEAH... WHY?
UGH...THIS ISN'T GOOD.
ERNIE IS YOUR AUNT'S OLD BOYFRIEND, AND HE IS A GRADE-A CREEP.
I ALWAYS WANTED TO PUNCH HIM IN THE FACE.
WHY DIDN'T YOU?
OH...
YOUR MOM BEAT ME TO IT.

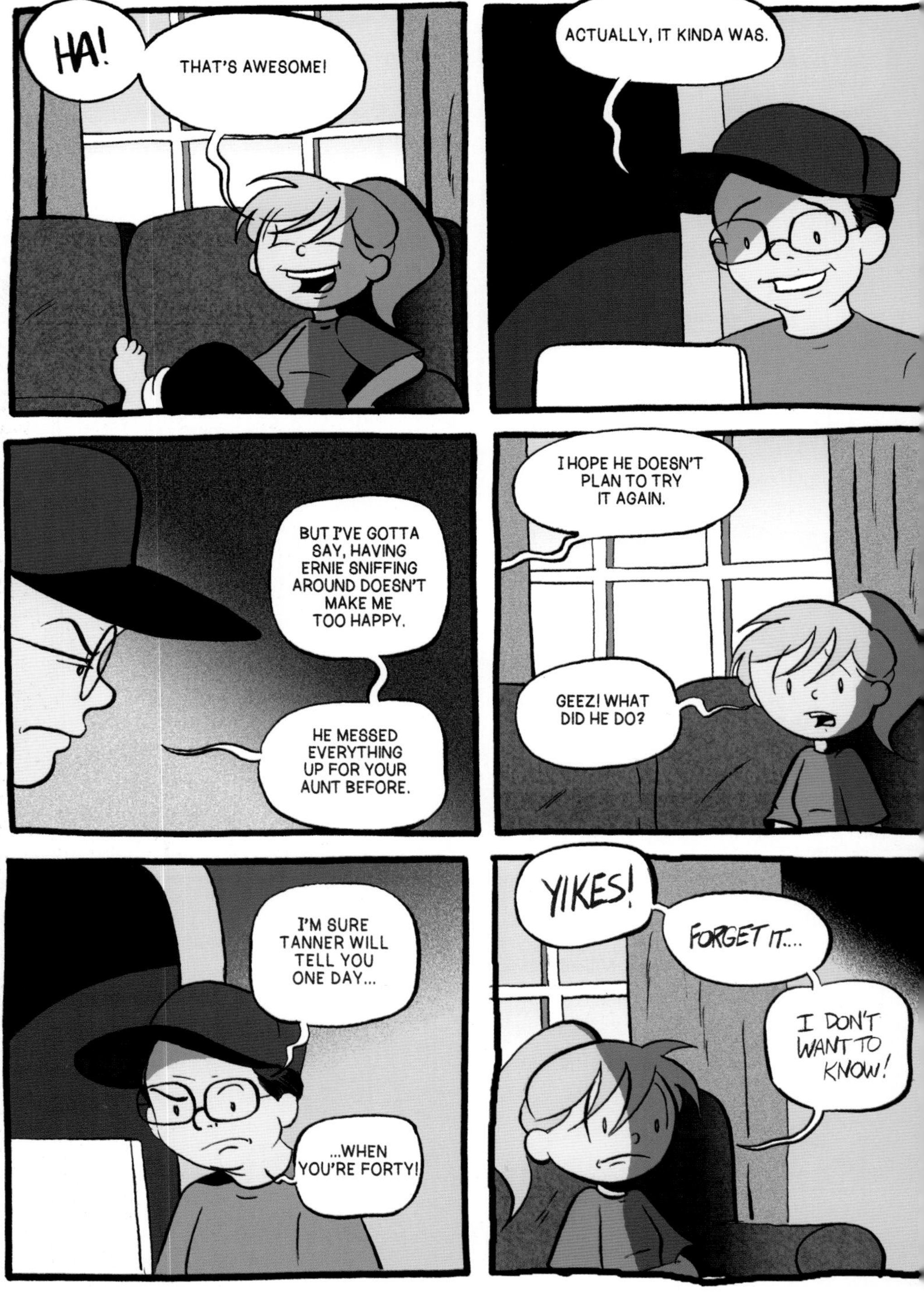
HA!
THAT'S AWESOME!
ACTUALLY, IT KINDA WAS.
BUT I'VE GOTTA SAY, HAVING ERNIE SNIFFING AROUND DOESN'T MAKE ME TOO HAPPY.
HE MESSED EVERYTHING UP FOR YOUR AUNT BEFORE.
I HOPE HE DOESN'T PLAN TO TRY IT AGAIN.
GEEZ! WHAT DID HE DO?
I'M SURE TANNER WILL TELL YOU ONE DAY...
...WHEN YOU'RE FORTY!
YIKES!
FORGET IT....
I DON'T WANT TO KNOW!

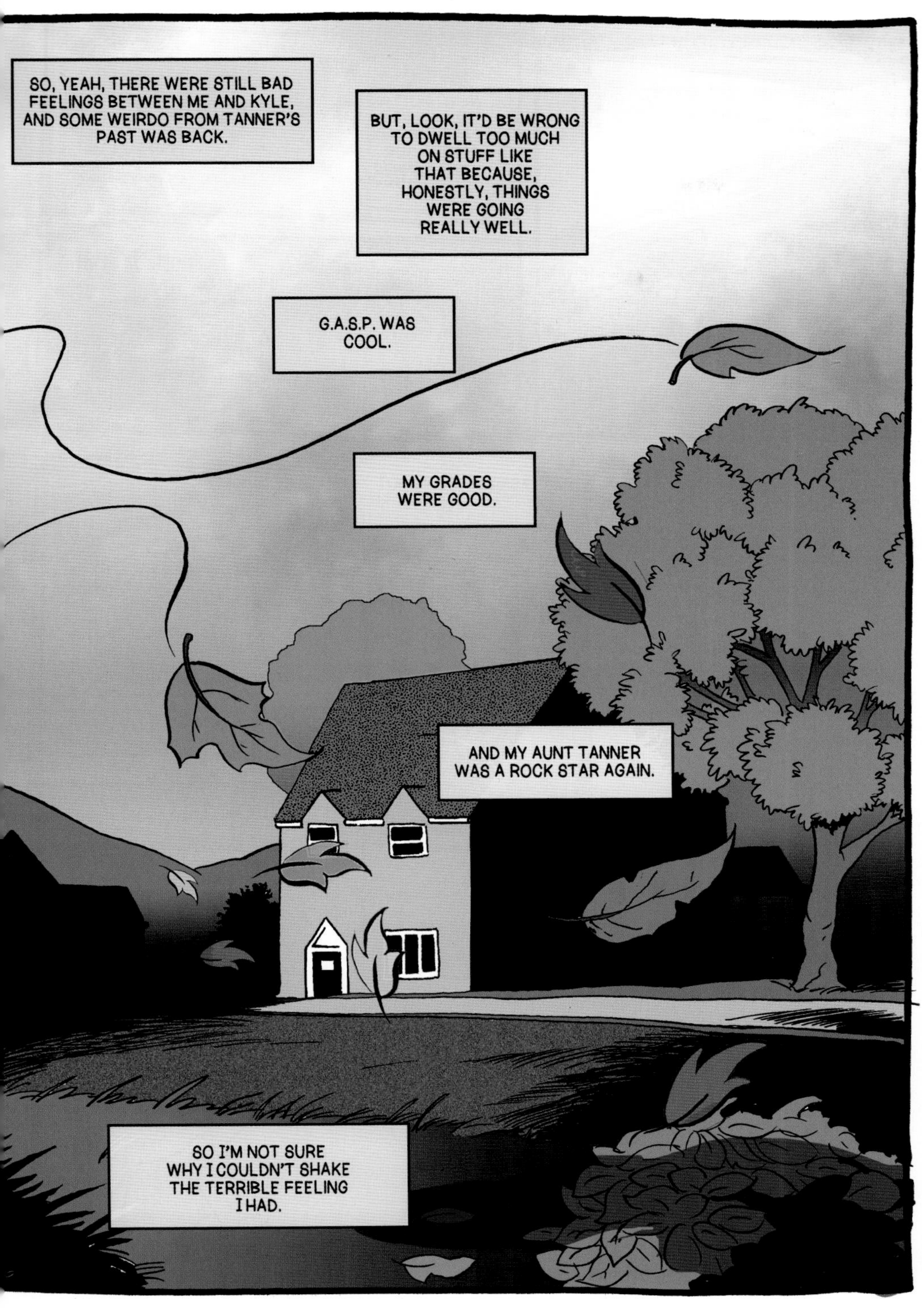
SO, YEAH, THERE WERE STILL BAD FEELINGS BETWEEN ME AND KYLE, AND SOME WEIRDO FROM TANNER'S PAST WAS BACK.
BUT, LOOK, IT'D BE WRONG TO DWELL TOO MUCH ON STUFF LIKE THAT BECAUSE, HONESTLY, THINGS WERE GOING REALLY WELL.
G.A.S.P. WAS COOL.
MY GRADES WERE GOOD.
AND MY AUNT TANNER WAS A ROCK STAR AGAIN.
SO I'M NOT SURE WHY I COULDN'T SHAKE THE TERRIBLE FEELING I HAD.

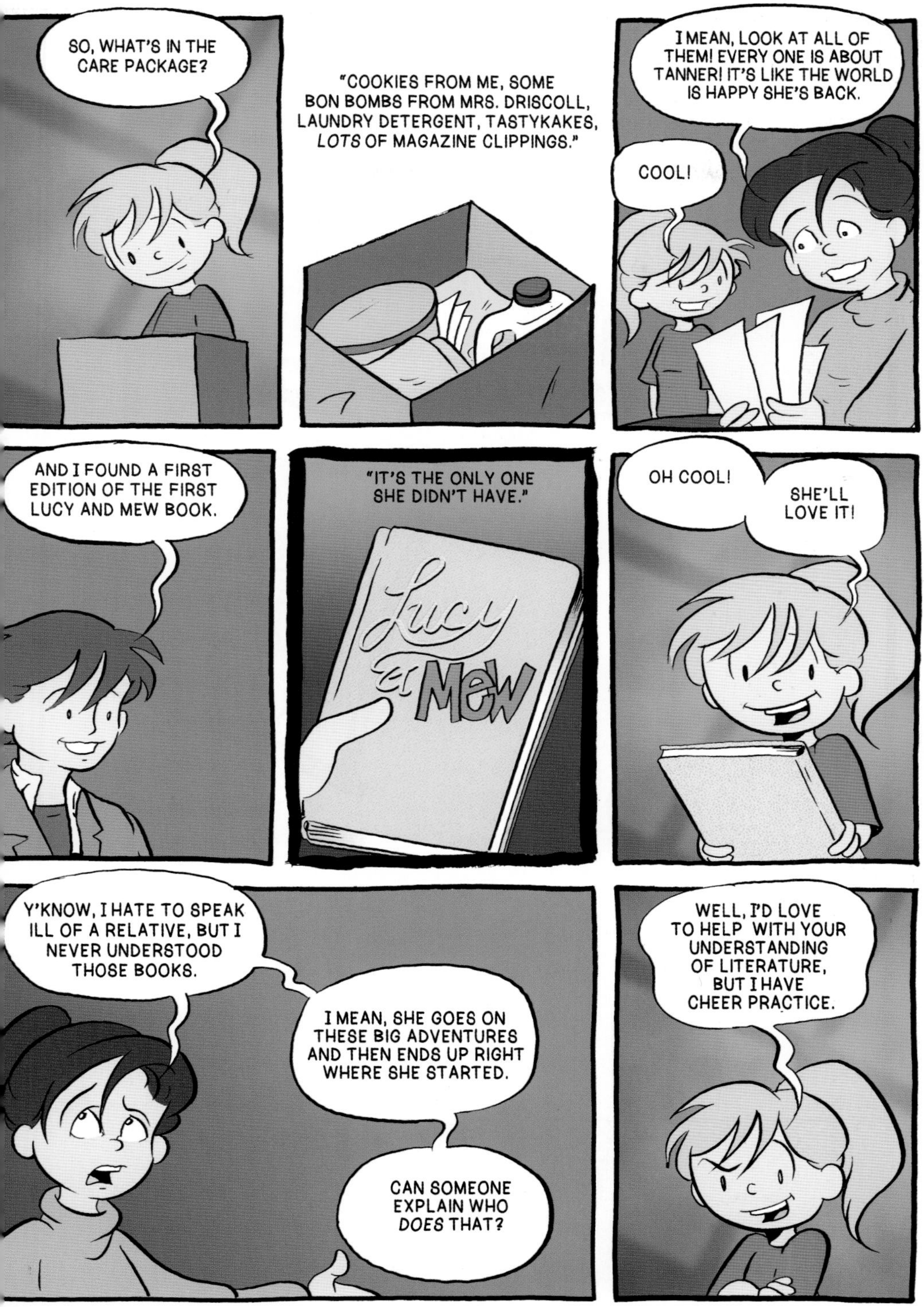
SO, WHAT'S IN THE CARE PACKAGE?
"COOKIES FROM ME, SOME BON BOMBS FROM MRS. DRISCOLL, LAUNDRY DETERGENT, TASTYKAKES, *LOTS* OF MAGAZINE CLIPPINGS."
I MEAN, LOOK AT ALL OF THEM! EVERY ONE IS ABOUT TANNER! IT'S LIKE THE WORLD IS HAPPY SHE'S BACK.
COOL!
AND I FOUND A FIRST EDITION OF THE FIRST LUCY AND MEW BOOK.
"IT'S THE ONLY ONE SHE DIDN'T HAVE."
Lucy & Mew
OH COOL!
SHE'LL LOVE IT!
Y'KNOW, I HATE TO SPEAK ILL OF A RELATIVE, BUT I NEVER UNDERSTOOD THOSE BOOKS.
I MEAN, SHE GOES ON THESE BIG ADVENTURES AND THEN ENDS UP RIGHT WHERE SHE STARTED.
CAN SOMEONE EXPLAIN WHO *DOES* THAT?
WELL, I'D LOVE TO HELP WITH YOUR UNDERSTANDING OF LITERATURE, BUT I HAVE CHEER PRACTICE.

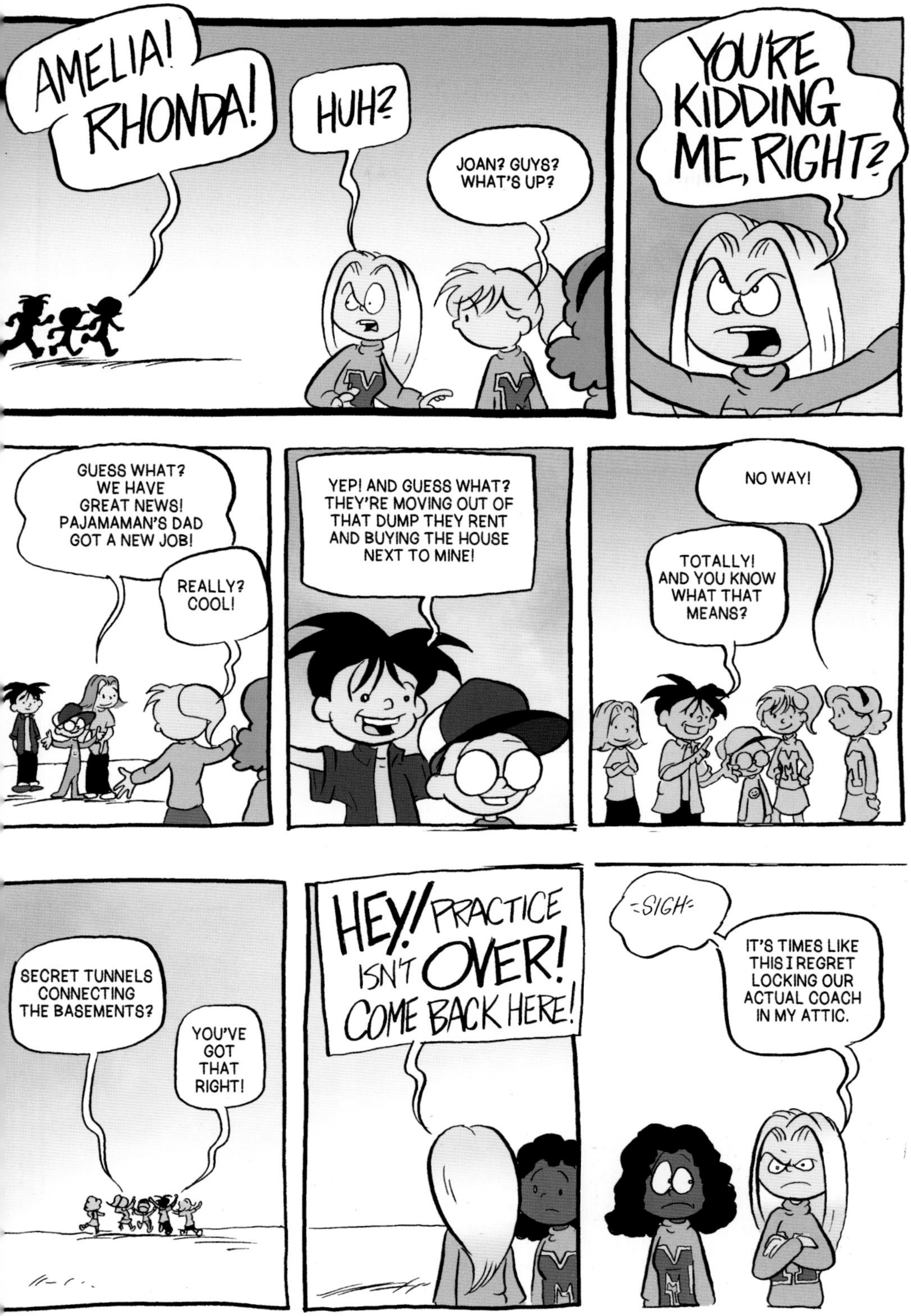
AMELIA! RHONDA!
HUH?
JOAN? GUYS? WHAT'S UP?
YOU'RE KIDDING ME, RIGHT?
GUESS WHAT? WE HAVE GREAT NEWS! PAJAMAMAN'S DAD GOT A NEW JOB!
REALLY? COOL!
YEP! AND GUESS WHAT? THEY'RE MOVING OUT OF THAT DUMP THEY RENT AND BUYING THE HOUSE NEXT TO MINE!
NO WAY!
TOTALLY! AND YOU KNOW WHAT THAT MEANS?
SECRET TUNNELS CONNECTING THE BASEMENTS?
YOU'VE GOT THAT RIGHT!
HEY! PRACTICE ISN'T OVER! COME BACK HERE!
=SIGH=
IT'S TIMES LIKE THIS I REGRET LOCKING OUR ACTUAL COACH IN MY ATTIC.

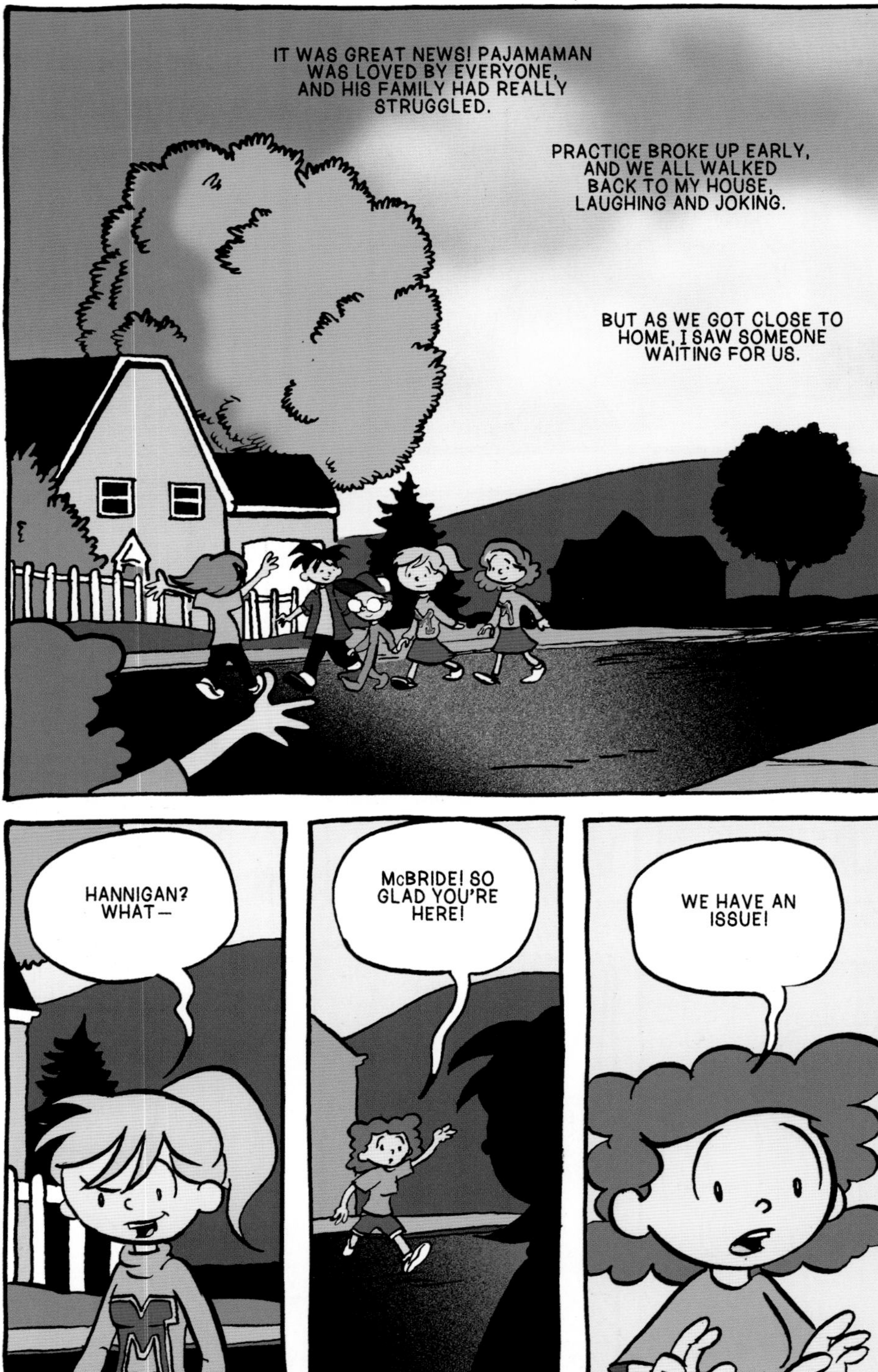
IT WAS GREAT NEWS! PAJAMAMAN WAS LOVED BY EVERYONE, AND HIS FAMILY HAD REALLY STRUGGLED.
PRACTICE BROKE UP EARLY, AND WE ALL WALKED BACK TO MY HOUSE, LAUGHING AND JOKING.
BUT AS WE GOT CLOSE TO HOME, I SAW SOMEONE WAITING FOR US.
HANNIGAN? WHAT—
McBRIDE! SO GLAD YOU'RE HERE!
WE HAVE AN ISSUE!

THAT WAS AN UNDERSTATEMENT. MY DAD WAS RIGHT TO WORRY ABOUT ERNIE. THIS TIME, HIS DESTRUCTION CAME IN THE FORM OF A TELL-ALL BOOK ABOUT TANNER. IT WAS STILL MONTHS AWAY FROM BEING PUBLISHED, BUT PARTS WERE ALREADY LEAKING ONLINE, AND EVERY LEAKED WORD WAS ANGRY AND HATEFUL AND JUST PLAIN MEAN.

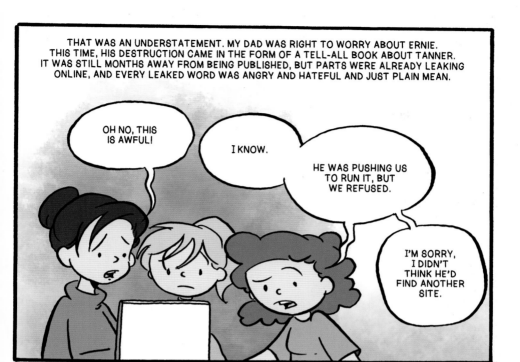

OH NO, THIS IS AWFUL!

I KNOW.

HE WAS PUSHING US TO RUN IT, BUT WE REFUSED.

I'M SORRY, I DIDN'T THINK HE'D FIND ANOTHER SITE.

JOANNE, NOW THAT THIS IS ON THIS WEBSITE, HOW FAST CAN IT SPREAD?

HONESTLY?

FAST.

65

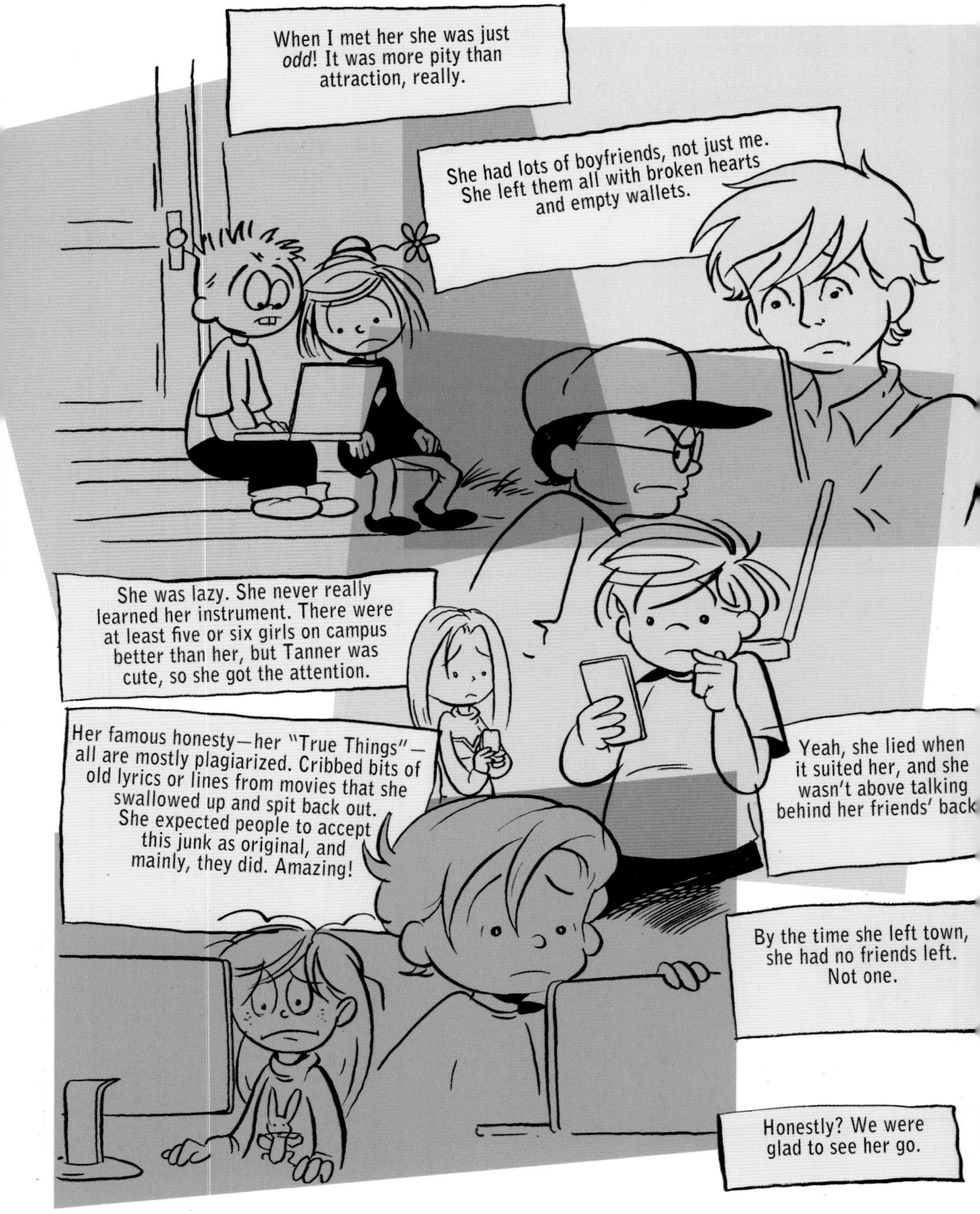

When I met her she was just *odd*! It was more pity than attraction, really.
She had lots of boyfriends, not just me. She left them all with broken hearts and empty wallets.
She was lazy. She never really learned her instrument. There were at least five or six girls on campus better than her, but Tanner was cute, so she got the attention.
Her famous honesty—her "True Things"—all are mostly plagiarized. Cribbed bits of old lyrics or lines from movies that she swallowed up and spit back out. She expected people to accept this junk as original, and mainly, they did. Amazing!
Yeah, she lied when it suited her, and she wasn't above talking behind her friends' back
By the time she left town, she had no friends left. Not one.
Honestly? We were glad to see her go.

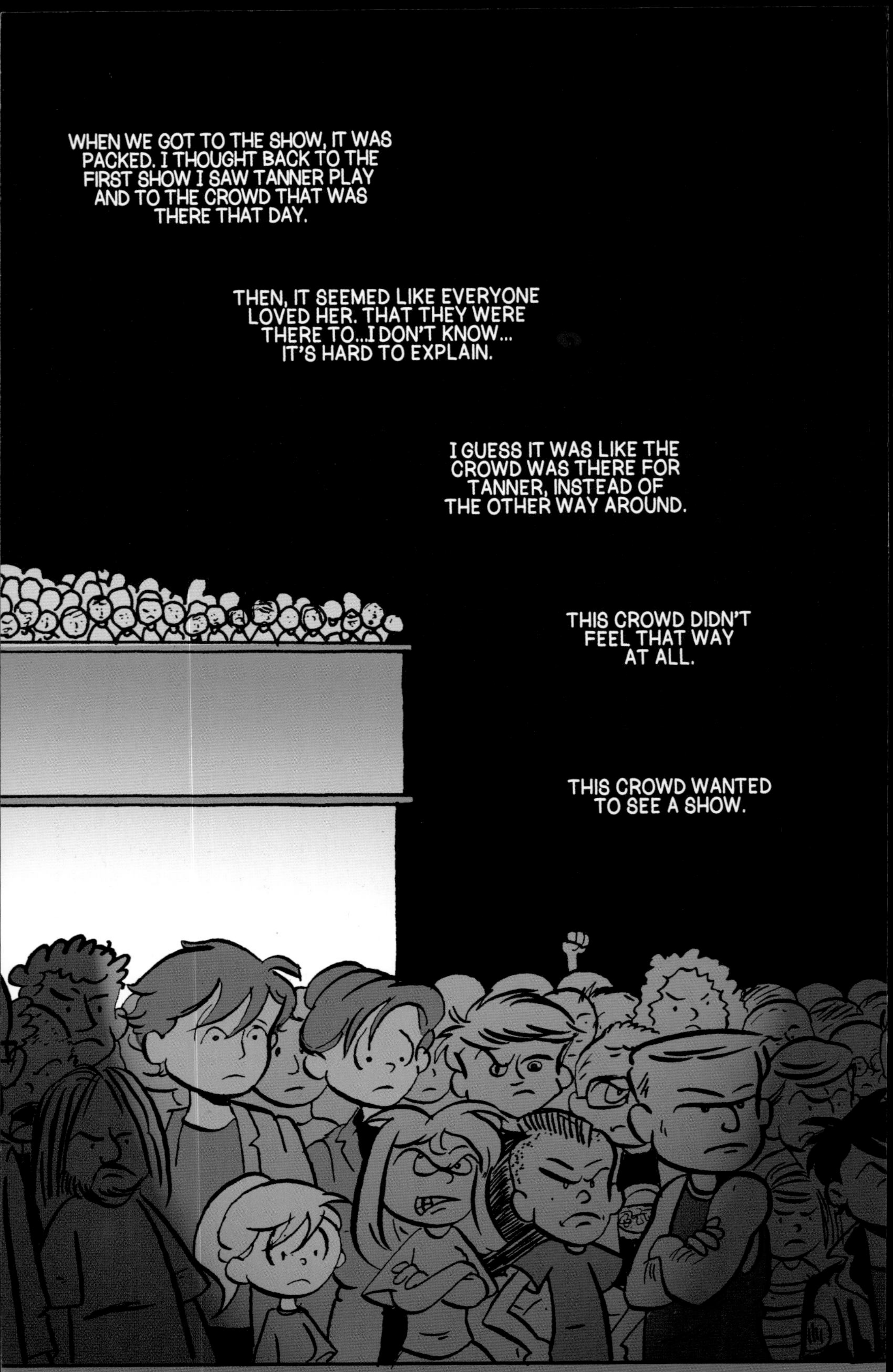
WHEN WE GOT TO THE SHOW, IT WAS PACKED. I THOUGHT BACK TO THE FIRST SHOW I SAW TANNER PLAY AND TO THE CROWD THAT WAS THERE THAT DAY.
THEN, IT SEEMED LIKE EVERYONE LOVED HER. THAT THEY WERE THERE TO...I DON'T KNOW... IT'S HARD TO EXPLAIN.
I GUESS IT WAS LIKE THE CROWD WAS THERE FOR TANNER, INSTEAD OF THE OTHER WAY AROUND.
THIS CROWD DIDN'T FEEL THAT WAY AT ALL.
THIS CROWD WANTED TO SEE A SHOW.

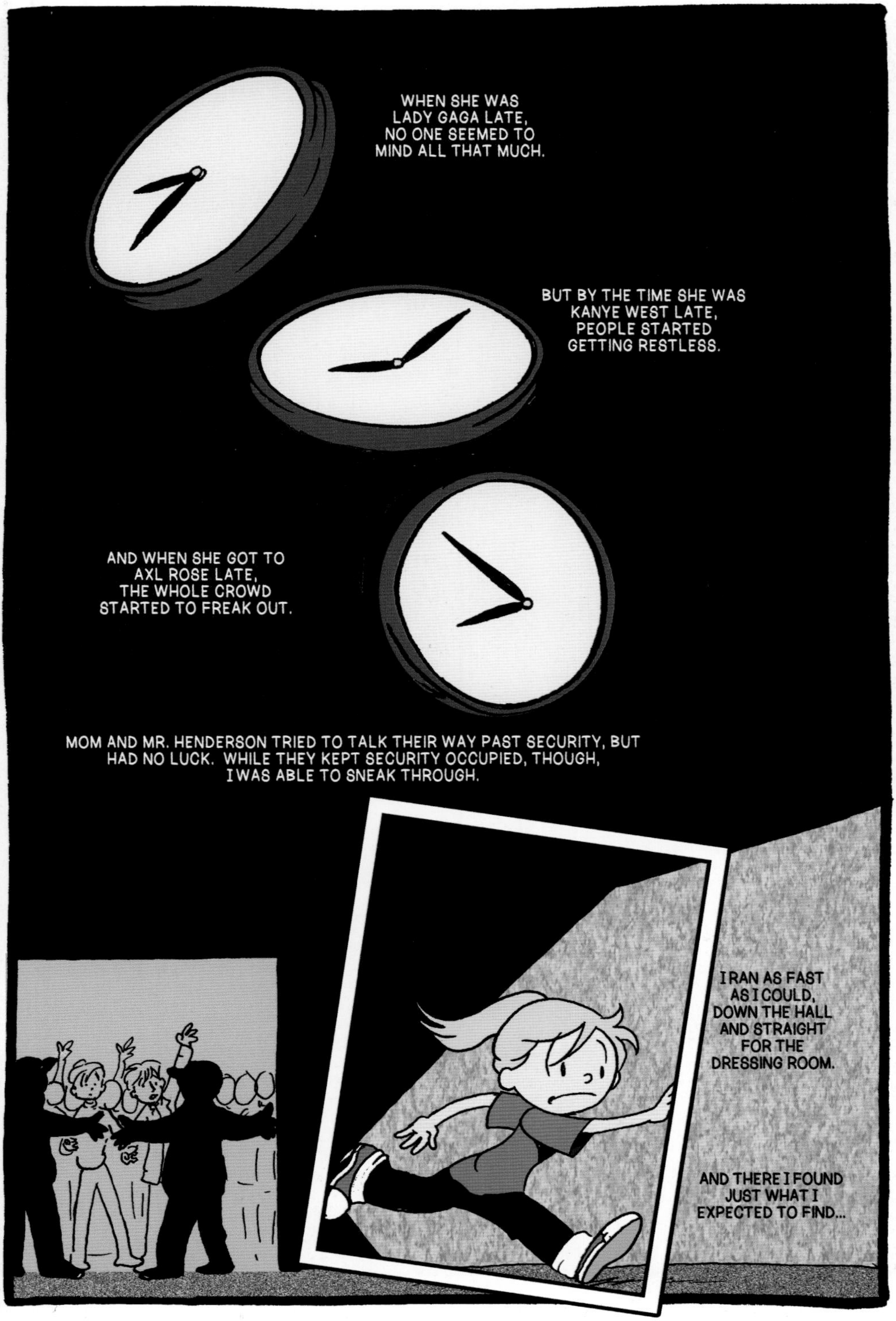
WHEN SHE WAS LADY GAGA LATE, NO ONE SEEMED TO MIND ALL THAT MUCH.
BUT BY THE TIME SHE WAS KANYE WEST LATE, PEOPLE STARTED GETTING RESTLESS.
AND WHEN SHE GOT TO AXL ROSE LATE, THE WHOLE CROWD STARTED TO FREAK OUT.
MOM AND MR. HENDERSON TRIED TO TALK THEIR WAY PAST SECURITY, BUT HAD NO LUCK. WHILE THEY KEPT SECURITY OCCUPIED, THOUGH, I WAS ABLE TO SNEAK THROUGH.
I RAN AS FAST AS I COULD, DOWN THE HALL AND STRAIGHT FOR THE DRESSING ROOM.
AND THERE I FOUND JUST WHAT I EXPECTED TO FIND...

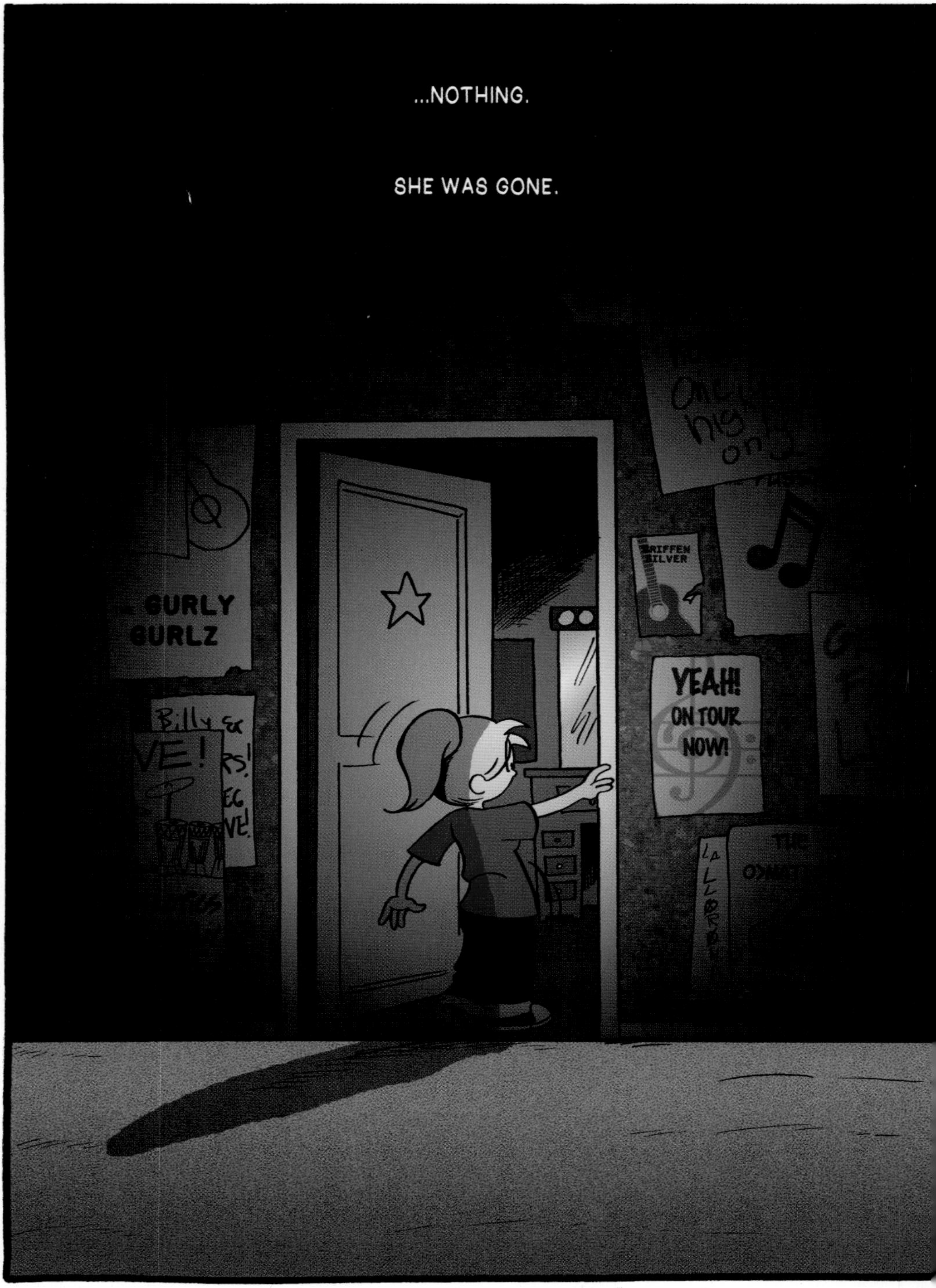
...NOTHING.
SHE WAS GONE.
GURLY GURLZ
GRIFFEN SILVER
YEAH! ON TOUR NOW!

IT WAS SHOCKING HOW SMOOTHLY
THE REST OF THE WORLD CARRIED
ON AFTER TANNER DISAPPEARED.

HOW COULD EVERYONE ELSE NOT
BE AS FREAKED OUT OR AS UPSET
AS I WAS?

BUT OTHER PEOPLE HAD
OTHER THINGS TO DEAL
WITH I GUESS.

AND BELIEVE IT OR NOT...

SOME OF IT WAS EVEN GOOD.

THE NEXT WEEKEND
WE ALL HELPED PAJAMAMAN
AND HIS FAMILY MOVE
INTO THEIR BEAUTIFUL
NEW HOME.

AND IT WAS GREAT, Y'KNOW? PM DESERVED TO BE HAPPY, AND I WAS AS HAPPY FOR HIM AS EVERYONE ELSE. BUT ALL I COULD THINK ABOUT WAS TANNER.

WHERE WAS SHE? HOW WAS SHE FEELING? WOULD I EVER SEE HER AGAIN?

AND MOSTLY, I WAS THINKING ABOUT HOW POWERLESS I FELT.

TOYS

WHEN SUDDENLY, I LOOKED INTO THE BOX I WAS CARRYING AND SAW SOMETHING THAT REMINDED ME I WASN'T POWERLESS.

THAT I COULD CHANGE THINGS FOR THE BETTER....

TOYS

AND I KNEW I HAD TO HELP HER.

I WENT TO MY ROOM, BUT NOT TO SLEEP. I WAS JUST SO ANGRY AND UPSET AND...I DON'T KNOW...I PRETTY MUCH FELT EVERYTHING, ALL AT ONCE.

SO I JUST SAT THERE GOING THROUGH THE UNSENT, AND NOW UNDELIVERED, CARE PACKAGE, STOPPING TO FLIP THROUGH THE LUCY AND MEW BOOK. AND AS I FLIPPED, I WATCHED THEM GO TO THE MOON. AND AROUND THE SUN AND TO THE NORTH POLE..." AND ALWAYS ALWAYS THEY END UP, NO MATTER HOW FAR THEY TRAVELED, RIGHT BACK WHERE THEY..." THE START.

T THE BEGINNING

BACK AGAIN.

HOME SAFE.

LIKE WE NEVER LEFT.

IN A CIRCLE.

WAIT!

79

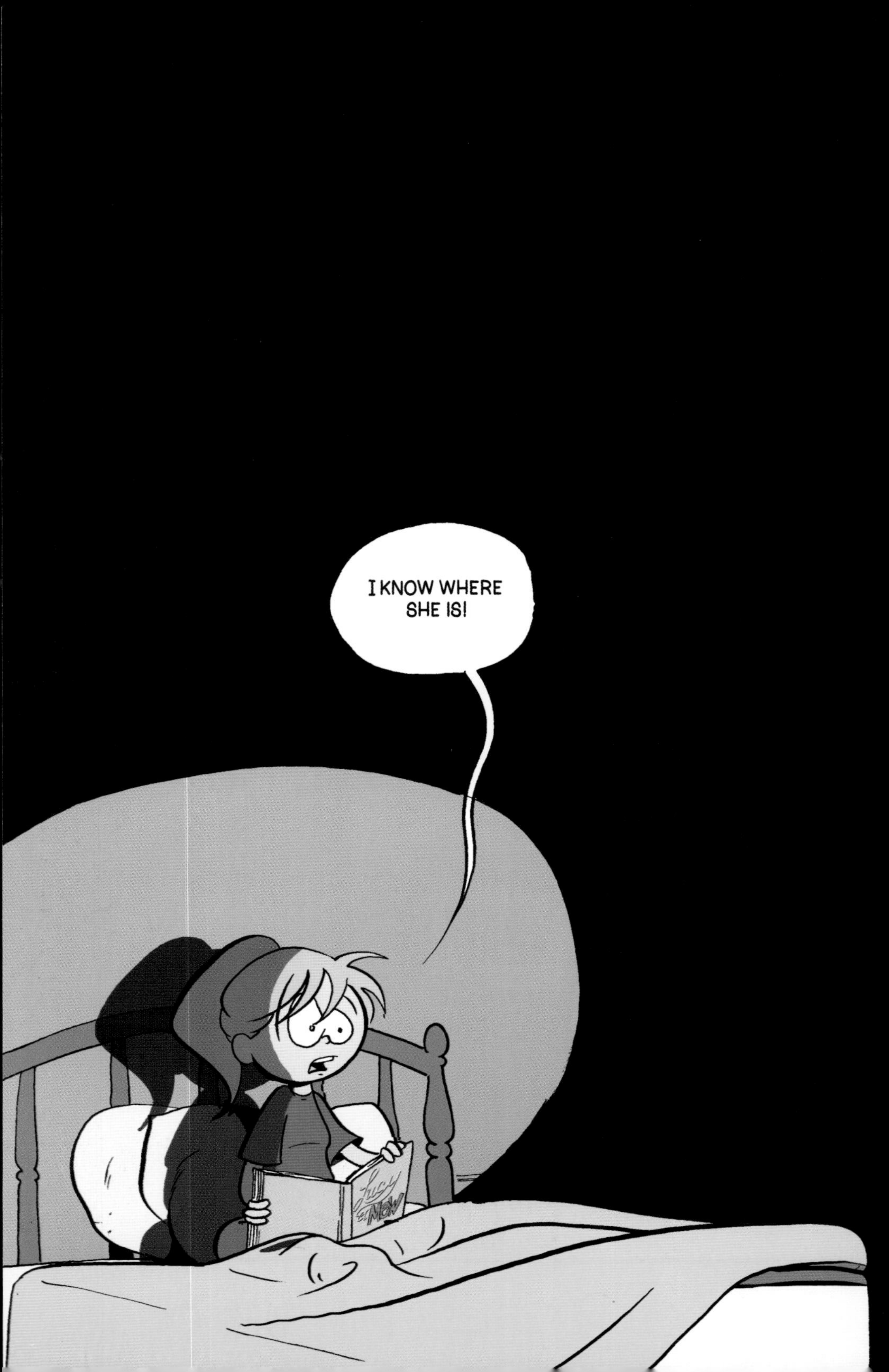
I KNOW WHERE SHE IS!

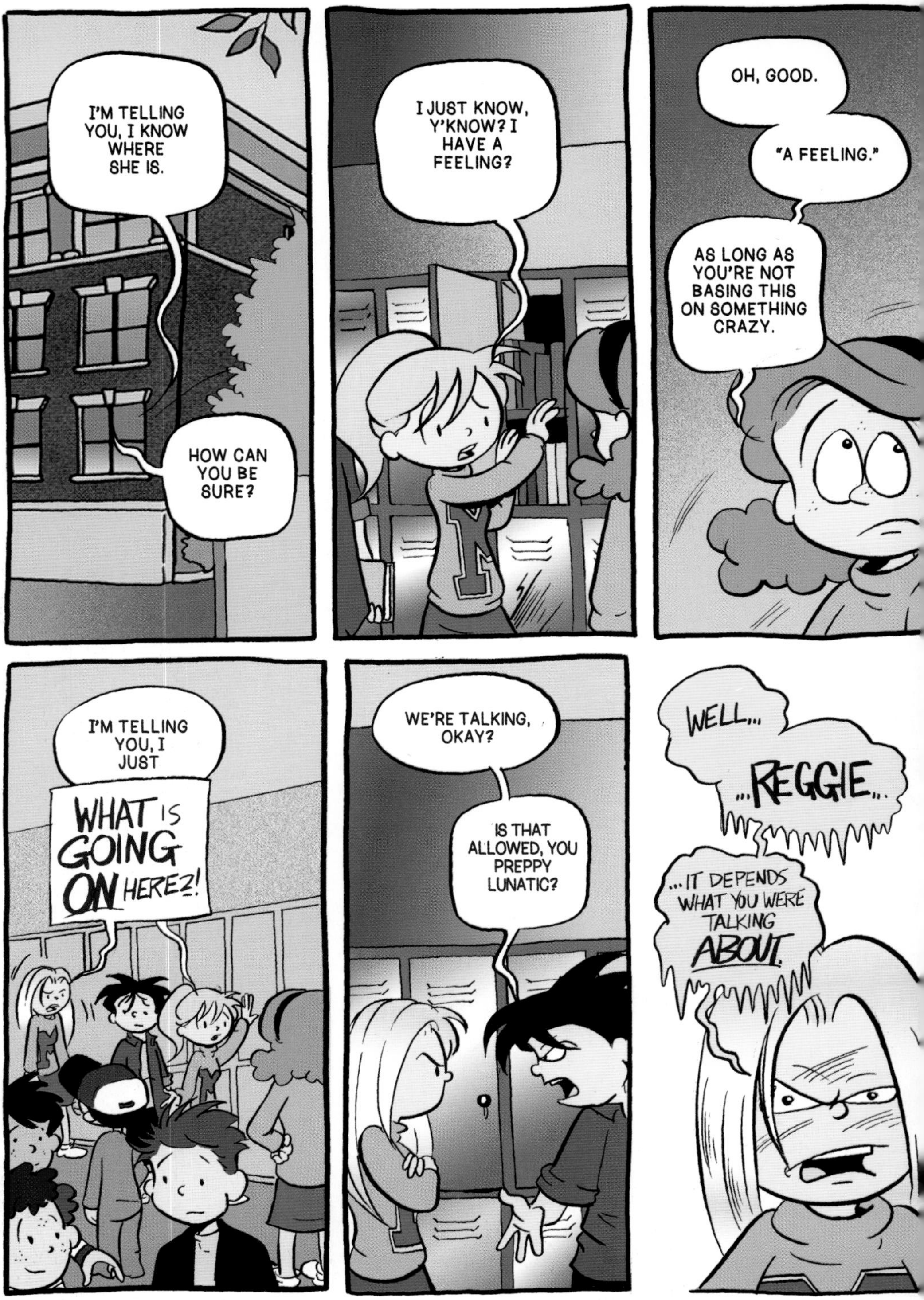
I'M TELLING YOU, I KNOW WHERE SHE IS.
HOW CAN YOU BE SURE?
I JUST KNOW, Y'KNOW? I HAVE A FEELING?
OH, GOOD.
"A FEELING."
AS LONG AS YOU'RE NOT BASING THIS ON SOMETHING CRAZY.
I'M TELLING YOU, I JUST
WHAT IS GOING ON HERE?!
WE'RE TALKING, OKAY?
IS THAT ALLOWED, YOU PREPPY LUNATIC?
WELL... ...REGGIE...
...IT DEPENDS WHAT YOU WERE TALKING ABOUT.

83

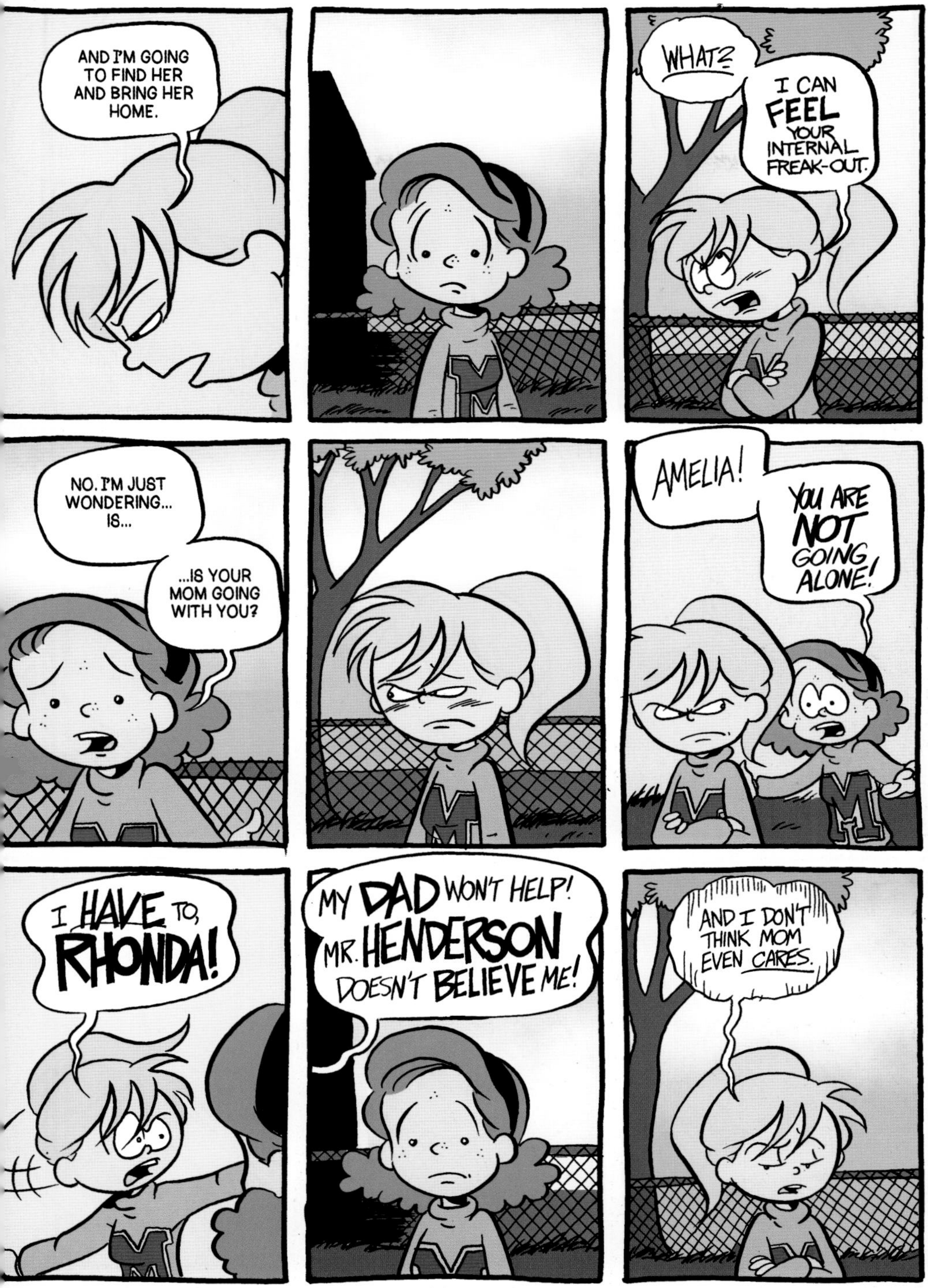
AND I'M GOING TO FIND HER AND BRING HER HOME.
WHAT?
I CAN FEEL YOUR INTERNAL FREAK-OUT.
NO. I'M JUST WONDERING... IS...
...IS YOUR MOM GOING WITH YOU?
AMELIA!
YOU ARE NOT GOING ALONE!
I HAVE TO, RHONDA!
MY DAD WON'T HELP! MR. HENDERSON DOESN'T BELIEVE ME!
AND I DON'T THINK MOM EVEN CARES.

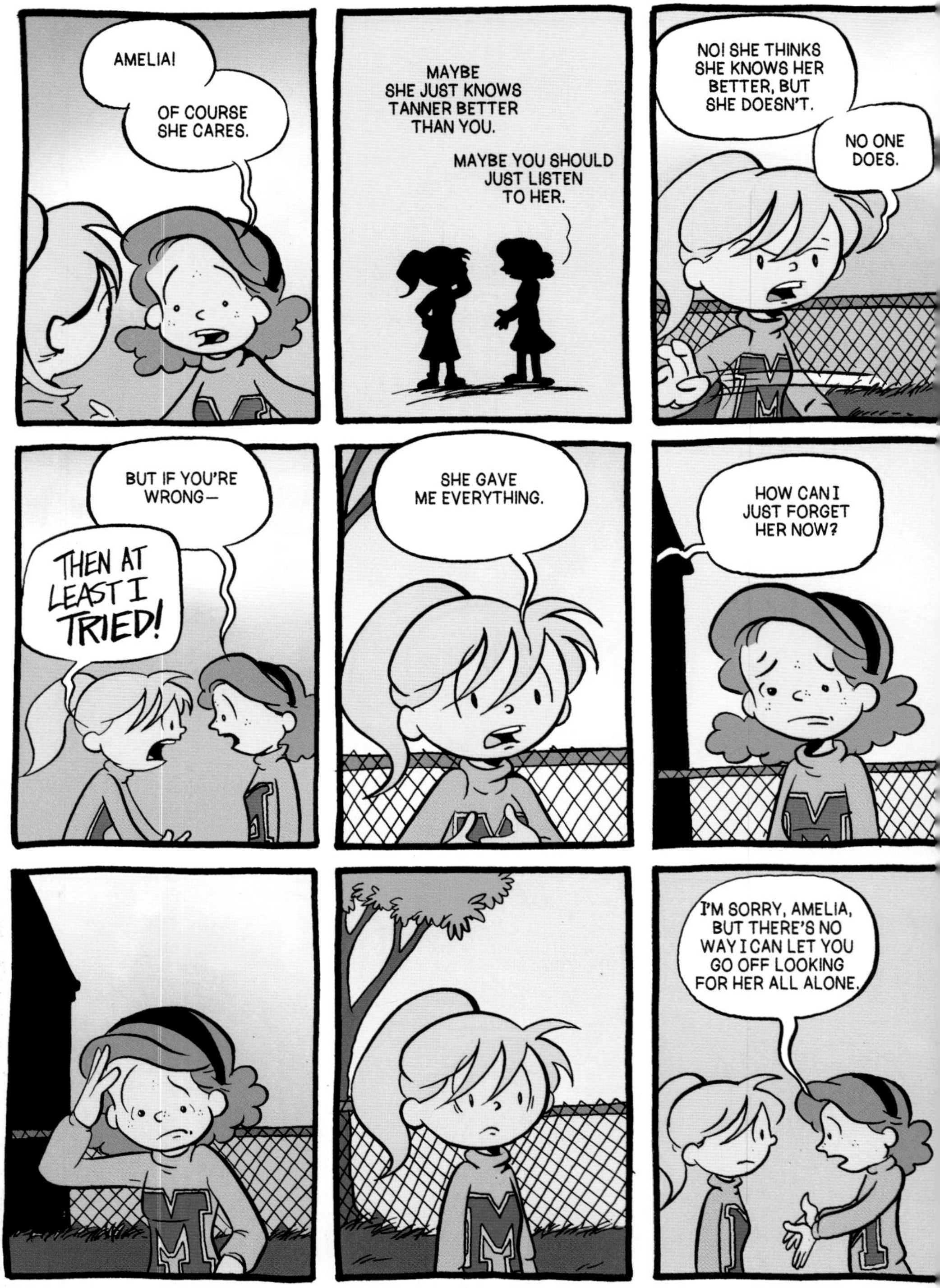
AMELIA!
OF COURSE SHE CARES.
MAYBE SHE JUST KNOWS TANNER BETTER THAN YOU.
MAYBE YOU SHOULD JUST LISTEN TO HER.
NO! SHE THINKS SHE KNOWS HER BETTER, BUT SHE DOESN'T.
NO ONE DOES.
BUT IF YOU'RE WRONG—
THEN AT LEAST I TRIED!
SHE GAVE ME EVERYTHING.
HOW CAN I JUST FORGET HER NOW?
I'M SORRY, AMELIA, BUT THERE'S NO WAY I CAN LET YOU GO OFF LOOKING FOR HER ALL ALONE.

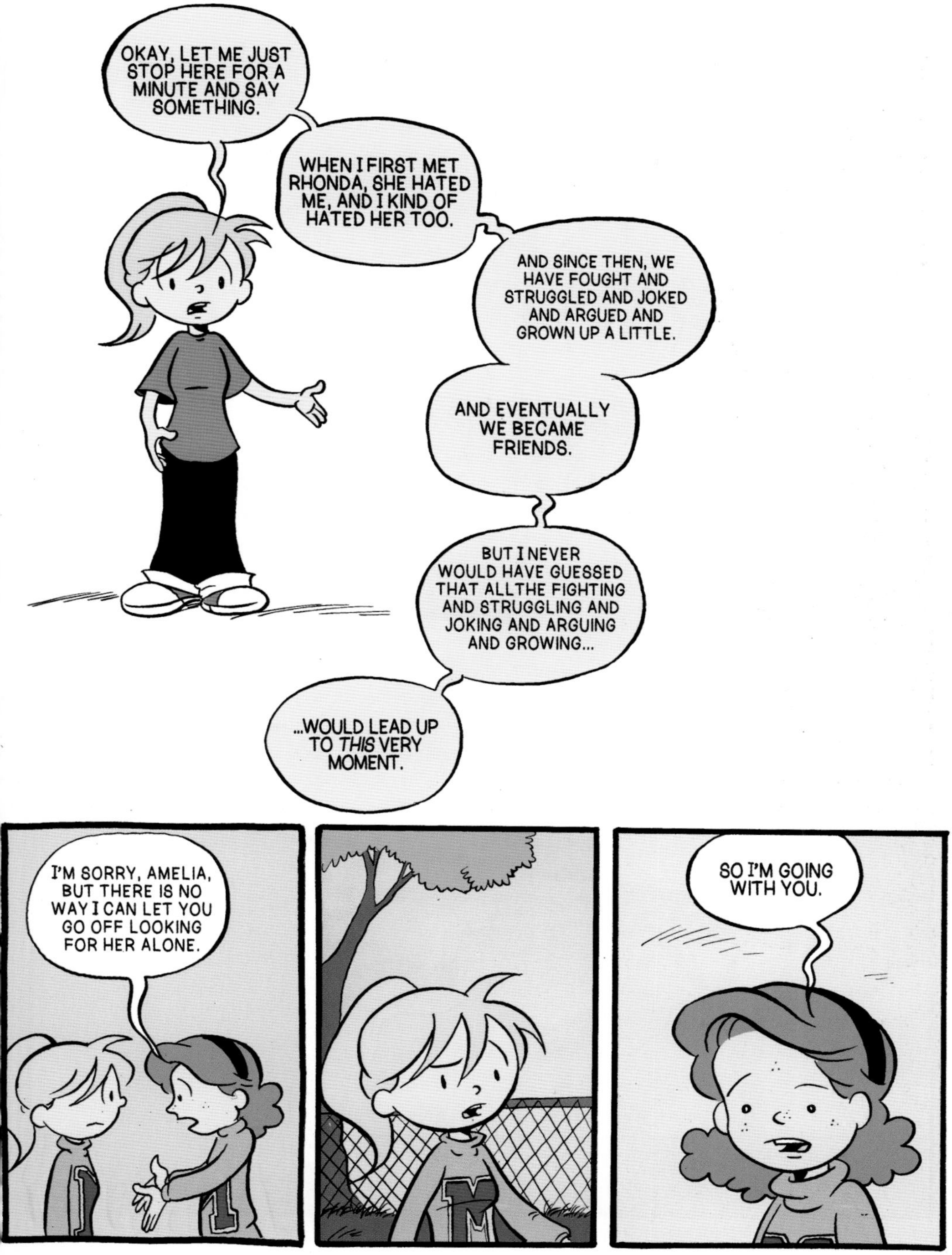
OKAY, LET ME JUST STOP HERE FOR A MINUTE AND SAY SOMETHING.
WHEN I FIRST MET RHONDA, SHE HATED ME, AND I KIND OF HATED HER TOO.
AND SINCE THEN, WE HAVE FOUGHT AND STRUGGLED AND JOKED AND ARGUED AND GROWN UP A LITTLE.
AND EVENTUALLY WE BECAME FRIENDS.
BUT I NEVER WOULD HAVE GUESSED THAT ALLTHE FIGHTING AND STRUGGLING AND JOKING AND ARGUING AND GROWING...
...WOULD LEAD UP TO *THIS* VERY MOMENT.
I'M SORRY, AMELIA, BUT THERE IS NO WAY I CAN LET YOU GO OFF LOOKING FOR HER ALONE.
SO I'M GOING WITH YOU.

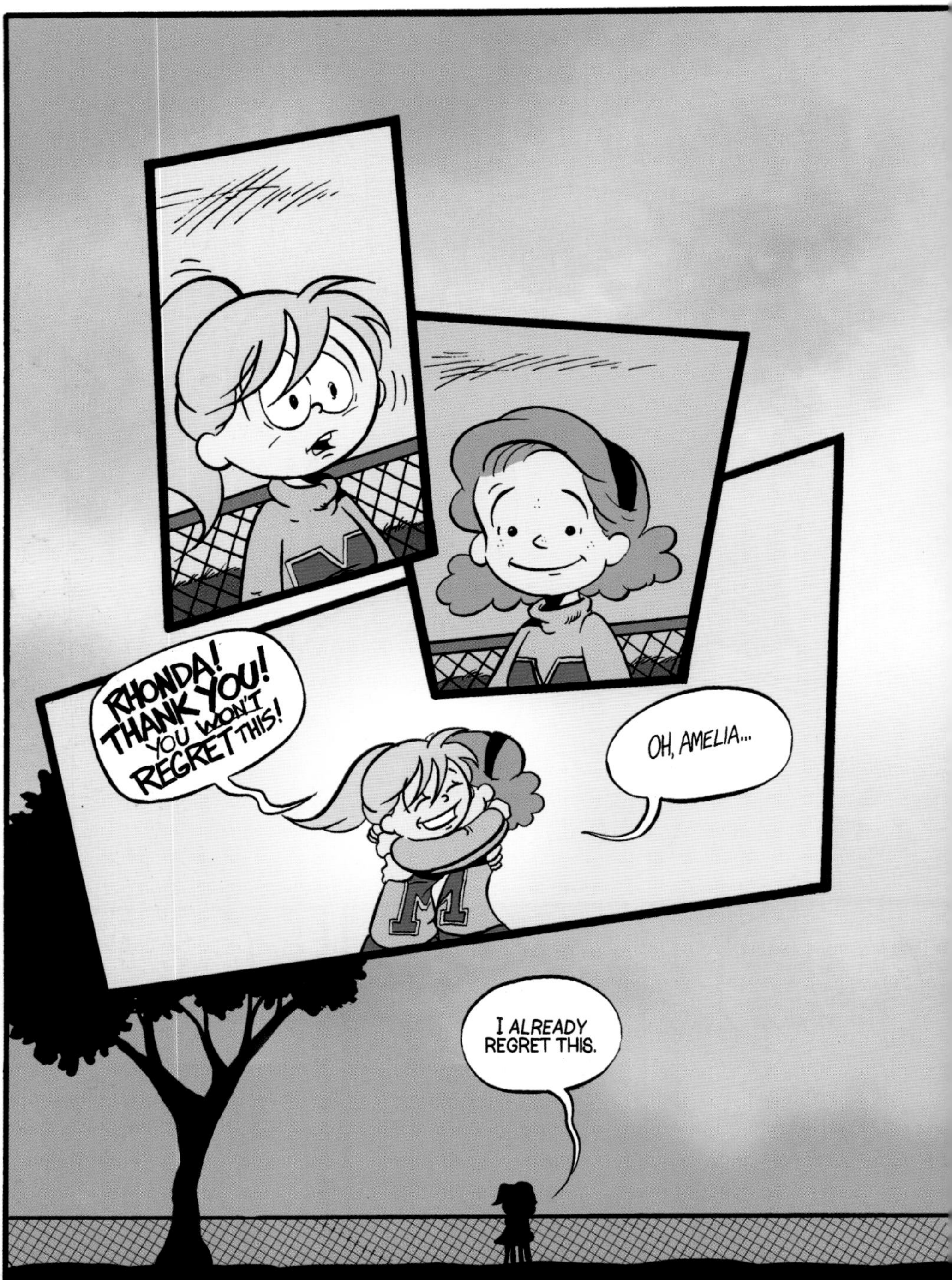
RHONDA! THANK YOU! YOU WON'T REGRET THIS!
OH, AMELIA...
I ALREADY REGRET THIS.

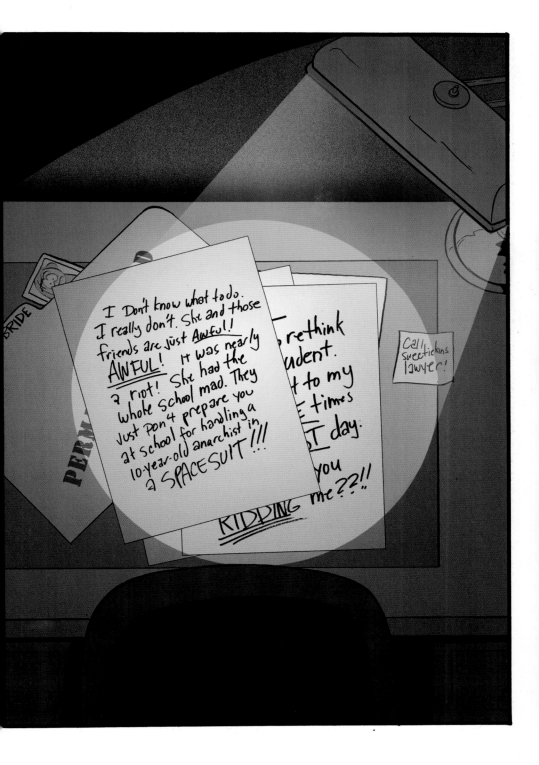

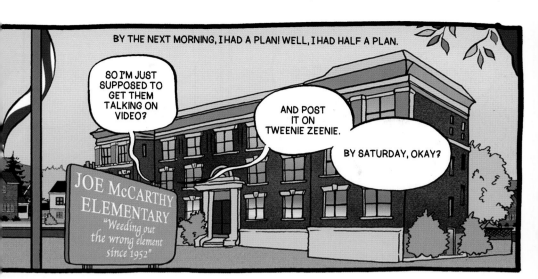

BY THE NEXT MORNING, I HAD A PLAN! WELL, I HAD HALF A PLAN.

SO I'M JUST SUPPOSED TO GET THEM TALKING ON VIDEO?

AND POST IT ON TWEENIE ZEENIE.

BY SATURDAY, OKAY?

JOE McCARTHY ELEMENTARY
"Weeding out the wrong element since 1952"

SATURDAY, GOT IT.

AND SPEAKING OF SATURDAY...

...THAT'S THE DAY OF THE CHEERLEADING COMPETITION. *YOU* NEED TO STOP IT.

STOP IT? HOW DO I DO THAT?

I DON'T KNOW. YOU'RE *YOU.*

DO SOMETHING YOU-ESQUE.

MISS McBRIDE!

CAN YOU SEE ME IN MY OFFICE?

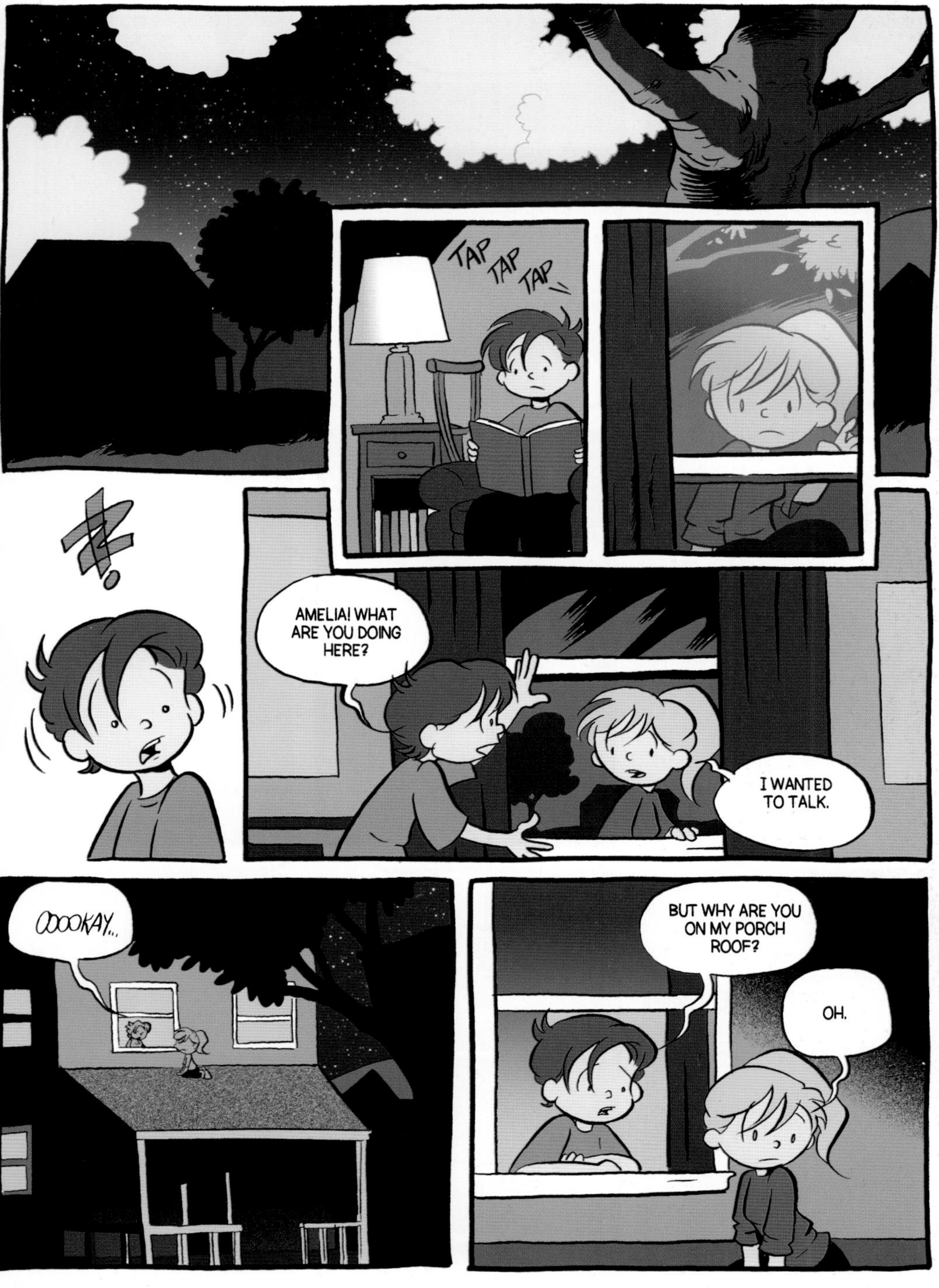
TAP TAP TAP
?!
AMELIA! WHAT ARE YOU DOING HERE?
I WANTED TO TALK.
OOOOKAY...
BUT WHY ARE YOU ON MY PORCH ROOF?
OH.

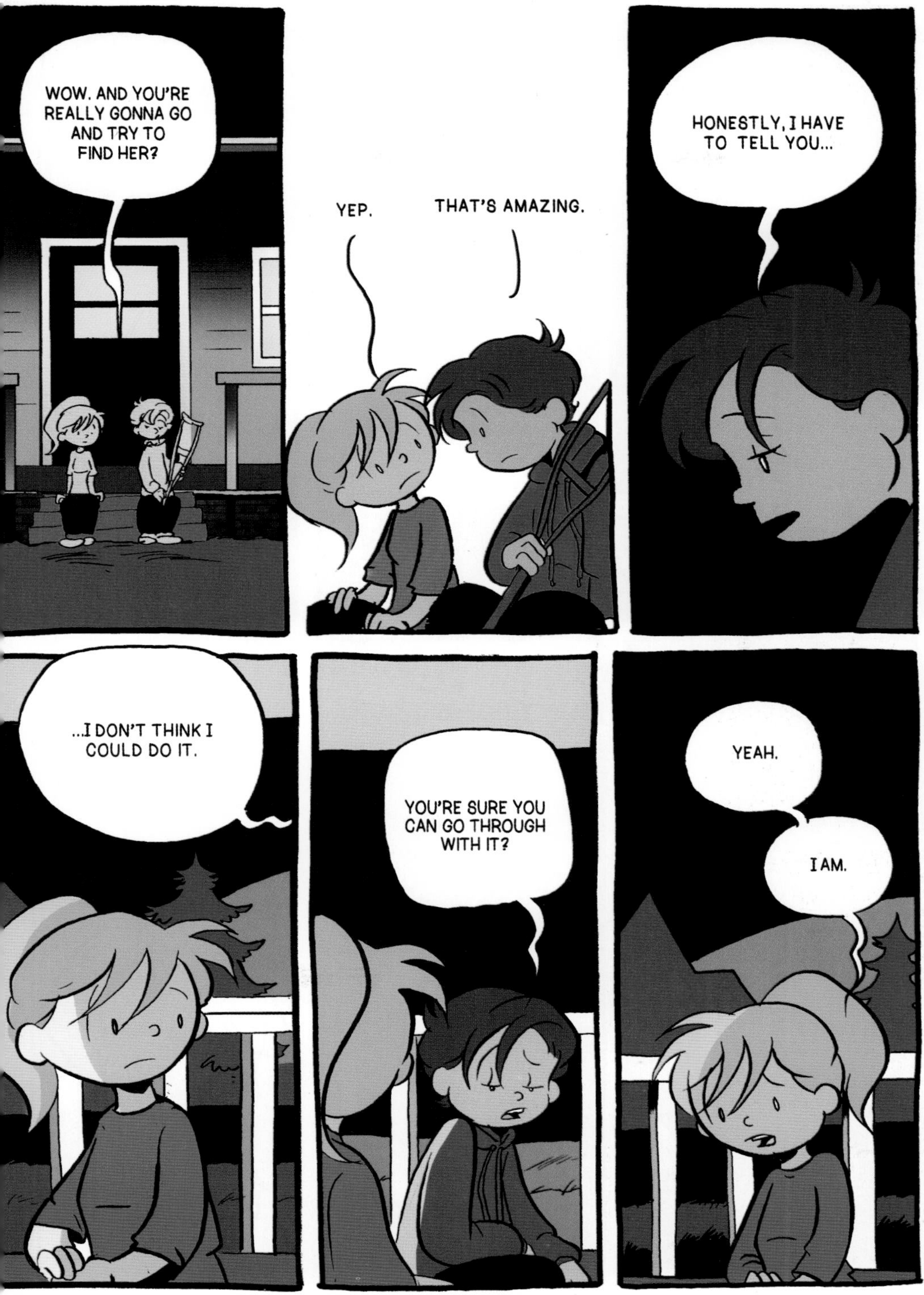
WOW. AND YOU'RE REALLY GONNA GO AND TRY TO FIND HER?
YEP.
THAT'S AMAZING.
HONESTLY, I HAVE TO TELL YOU...
...I DON'T THINK I COULD DO IT.
YOU'RE SURE YOU CAN GO THROUGH WITH IT?
YEAH.
I AM.

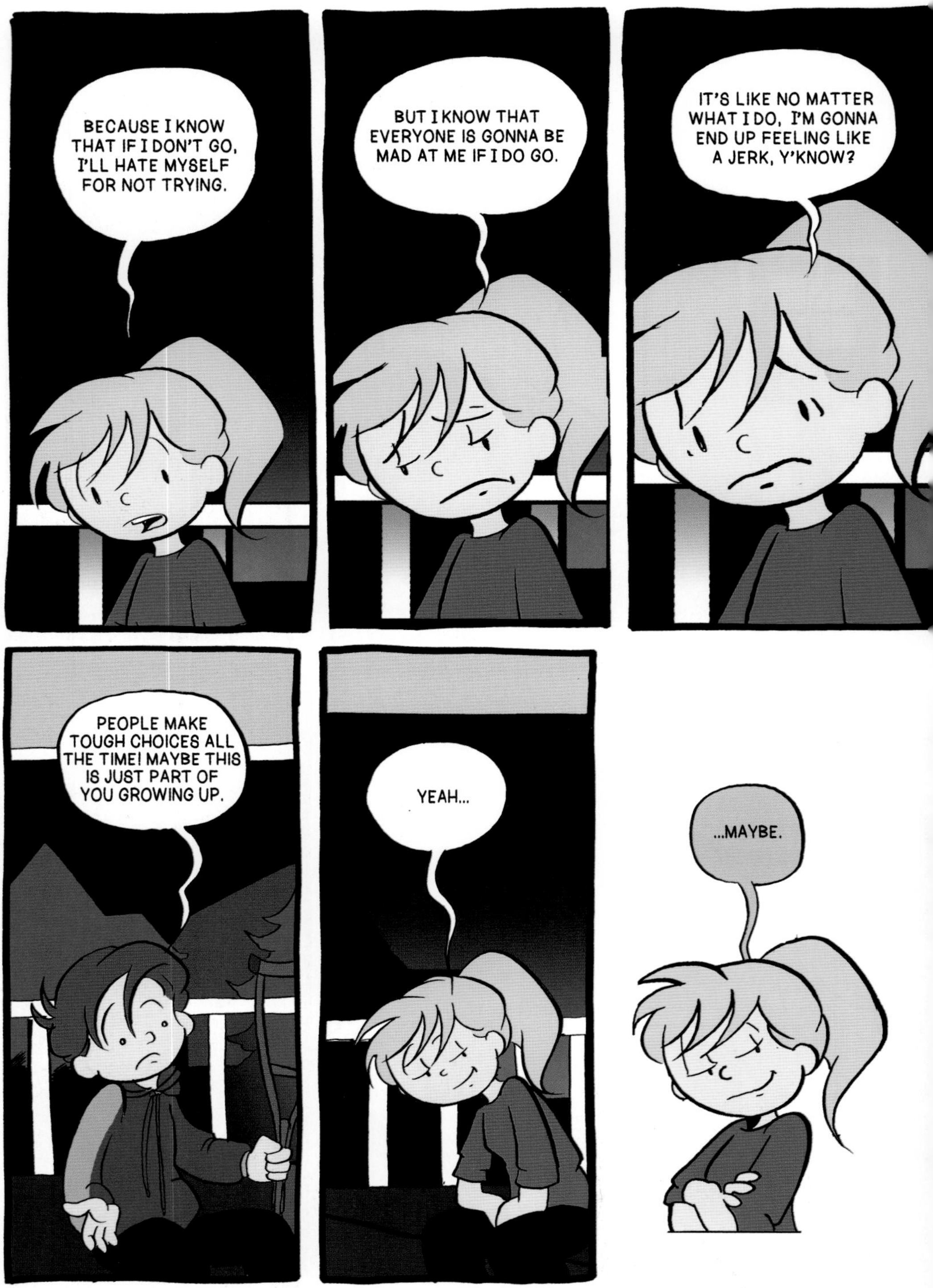
BECAUSE I KNOW THAT IF I DON'T GO, I'LL HATE MYSELF FOR NOT TRYING.
BUT I KNOW THAT EVERYONE IS GONNA BE MAD AT ME IF I DO GO.
IT'S LIKE NO MATTER WHAT I DO, I'M GONNA END UP FEELING LIKE A JERK, Y'KNOW?
PEOPLE MAKE TOUGH CHOICES ALL THE TIME! MAYBE THIS IS JUST PART OF YOU GROWING UP.
YEAH...
...MAYBE.

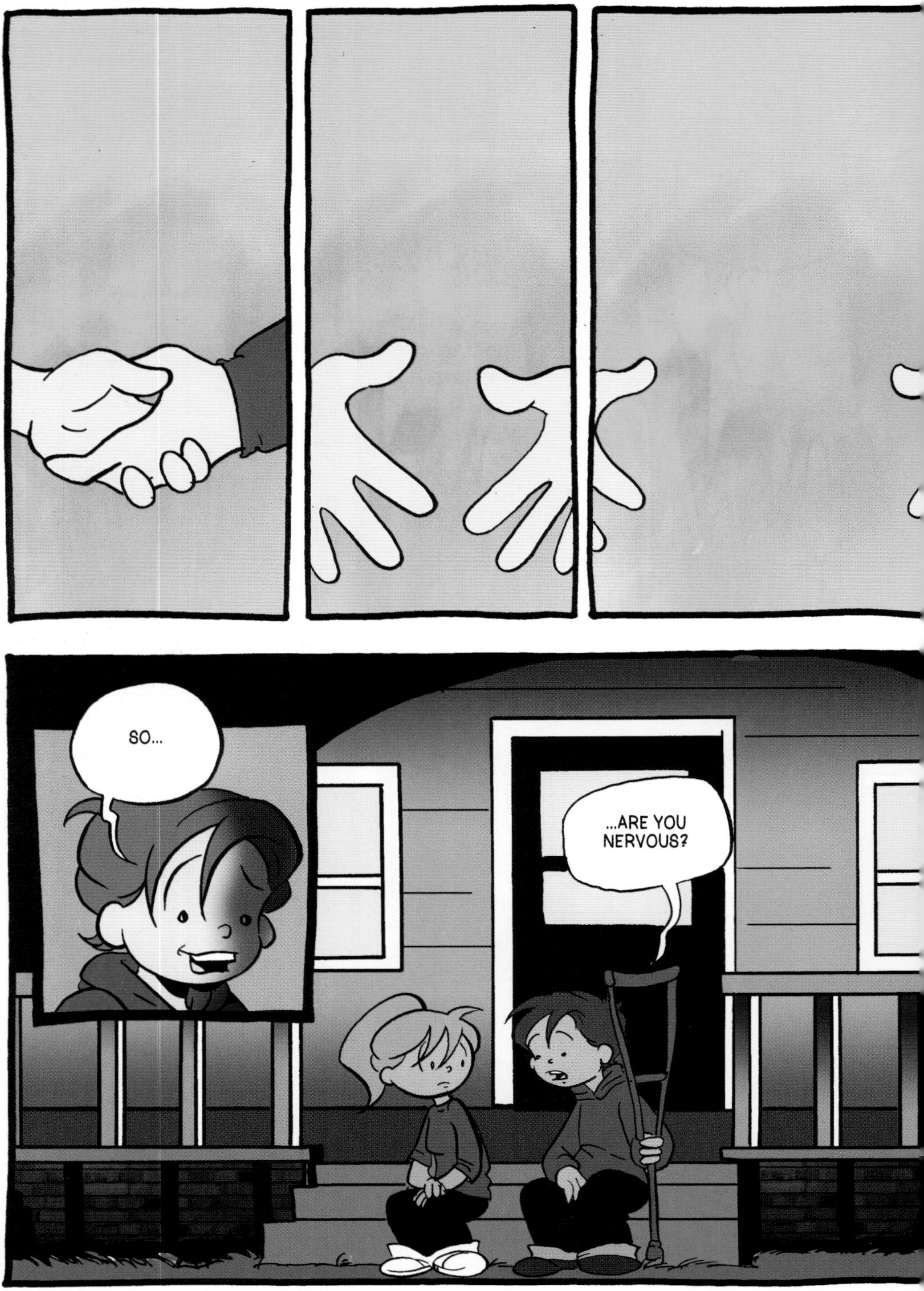
SO...
...ARE YOU NERVOUS?

ARE YOU KIDDING? I'M TERRIFIED!

I MEAN, WHAT IF I CAN'T FIND HER?

WHAT IF SHE DOESN'T WANT TO BE FOUND?

AND THERE'S MY PARENTS AND SCHOOL AND THE CHEERLEADING COMPETITION!

THIS IS THE CRAZIEST THING I'VE EVER DONE! BUT I HAVE TO DO IT, YKNOW? BUT I CAN'T TELL IF IT'S RIGHT OR WRONG OR WHAT?!

GAHHH!

SOMETIMES IT'S LIKE I DON'T KNOW WHO I AM ANYMORE!

ARE YOU KIDDING ME?

YOU'RE AMELIA McBRIDE!

THE NEXT NIGHT WE CONVENED AT THE CLUBHOUSE TO TRY TO COME UP WITH A PLAN.

WHAT IS HE DOING HERE?

REGGIE, I INVITED KYLE.

CAN YOU PLEASE JUST BE COOL?

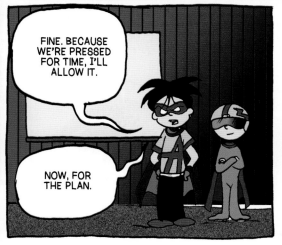

FINE. BECAUSE WE'RE PRESSED FOR TIME, I'LL ALLOW IT.

NOW, FOR THE PLAN.

PREPARE TO HAVE YOUR MINDS BLOWN.

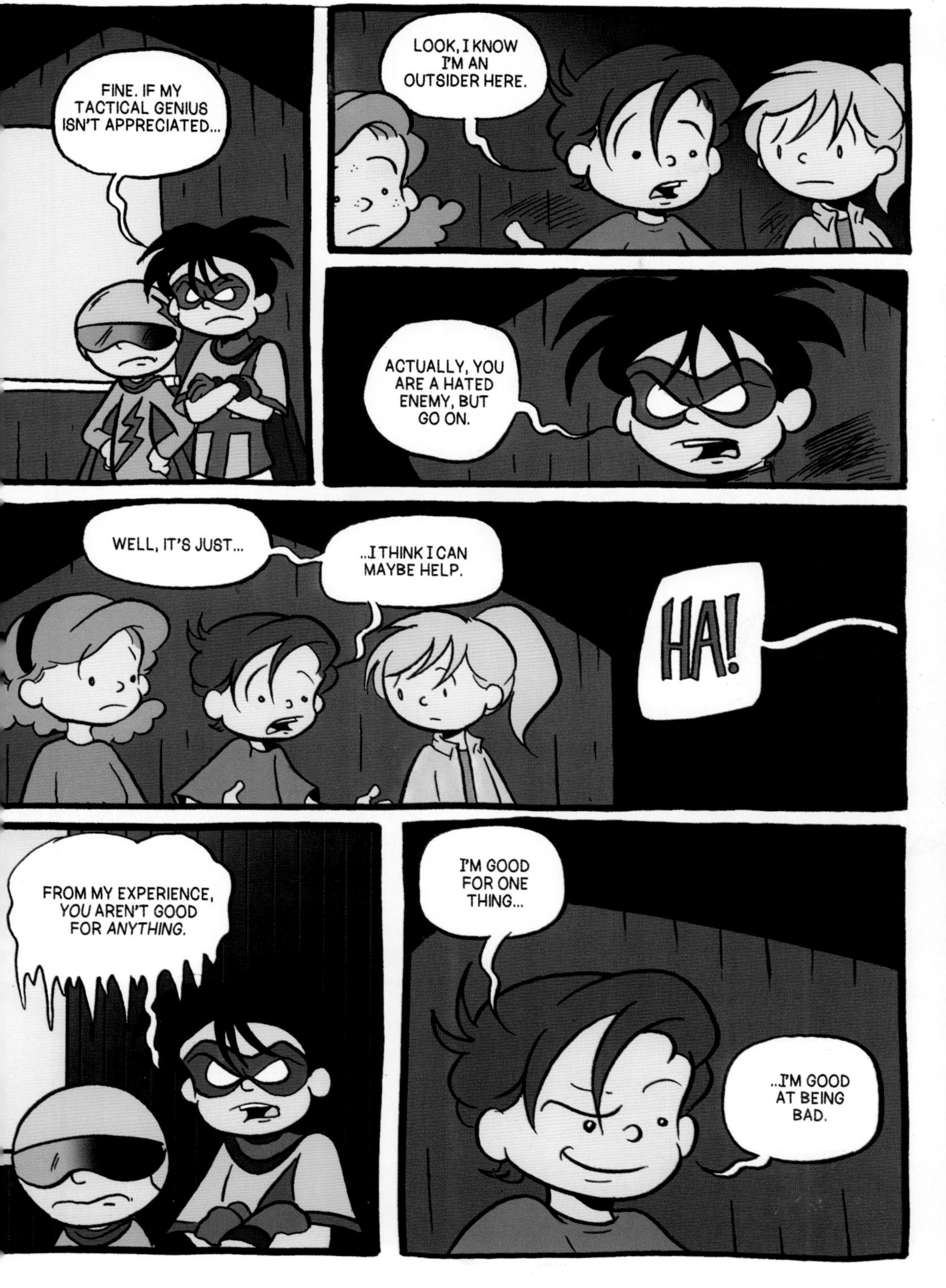
FINE. IF MY TACTICAL GENIUS ISN'T APPRECIATED...
LOOK, I KNOW I'M AN OUTSIDER HERE.
ACTUALLY, YOU ARE A HATED ENEMY, BUT GO ON.
WELL, IT'S JUST...
...I THINK I CAN MAYBE HELP.
HA!
FROM MY EXPERIENCE, *YOU* AREN'T GOOD FOR *ANYTHING.*
I'M GOOD FOR ONE THING...
...I'M GOOD AT BEING BAD.

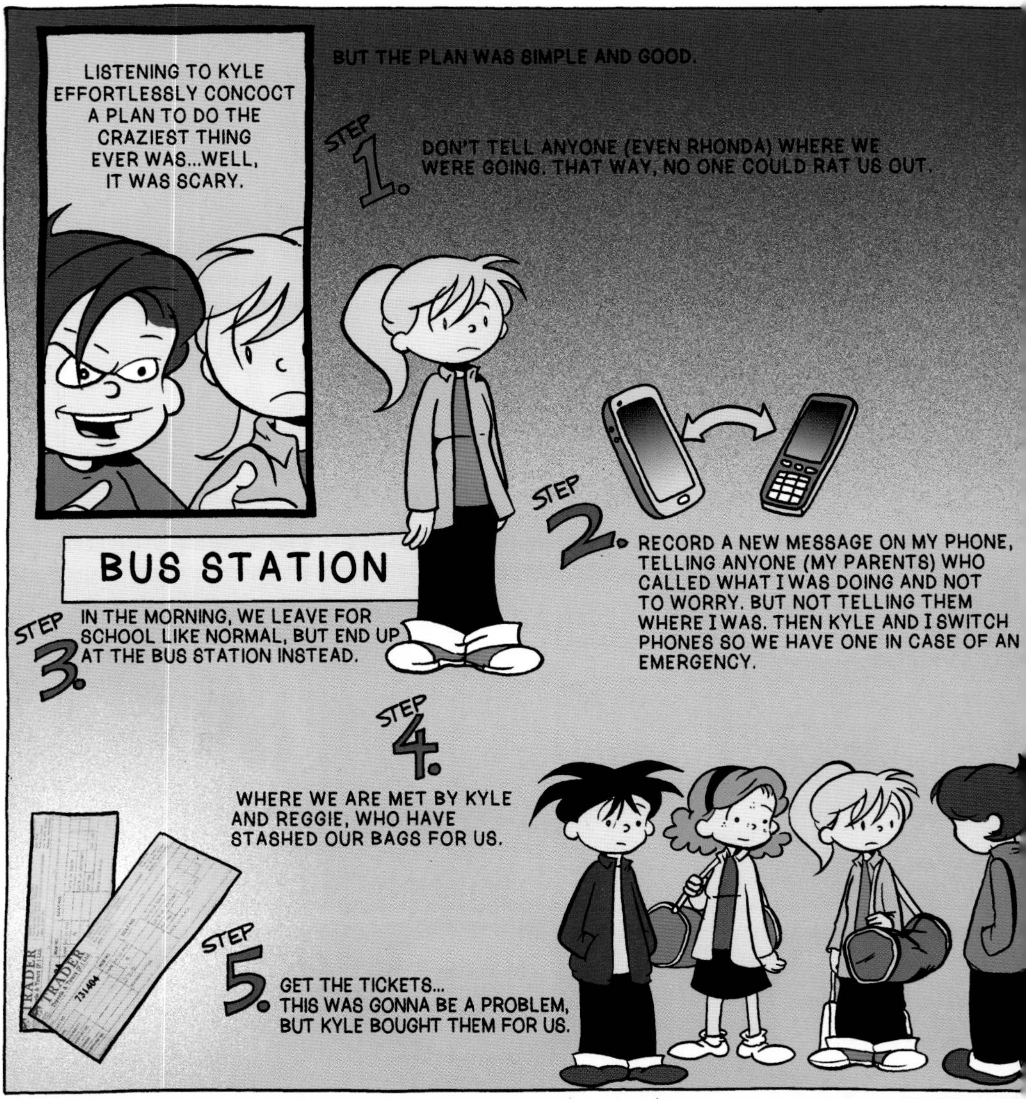
LISTENING TO KYLE EFFORTLESSLY CONCOCT A PLAN TO DO THE CRAZIEST THING EVER WAS...WELL, IT WAS SCARY.
BUT THE PLAN WAS SIMPLE AND GOOD.
STEP 1. DON'T TELL ANYONE (EVEN RHONDA) WHERE WE WERE GOING. THAT WAY, NO ONE COULD RAT US OUT.
STEP 2. RECORD A NEW MESSAGE ON MY PHONE, TELLING ANYONE (MY PARENTS) WHO CALLED WHAT I WAS DOING AND NOT TO WORRY. BUT NOT TELLING THEM WHERE I WAS. THEN KYLE AND I SWITCH PHONES SO WE HAVE ONE IN CASE OF AN EMERGENCY.
BUS STATION
STEP 3. IN THE MORNING, WE LEAVE FOR SCHOOL LIKE NORMAL, BUT END UP AT THE BUS STATION INSTEAD.
STEP 4. WHERE WE ARE MET BY KYLE AND REGGIE, WHO HAVE STASHED OUR BAGS FOR US.
STEP 5. GET THE TICKETS... THIS WAS GONNA BE A PROBLEM, BUT KYLE BOUGHT THEM FOR US.

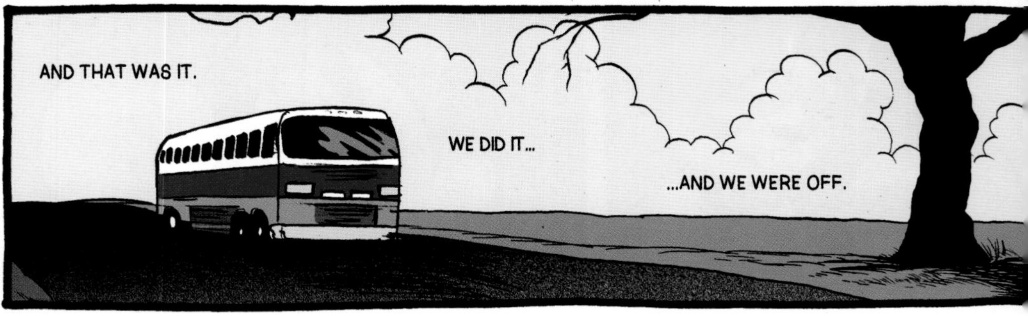
AND THAT WAS IT.
WE DID IT...
...AND WE WERE OFF.

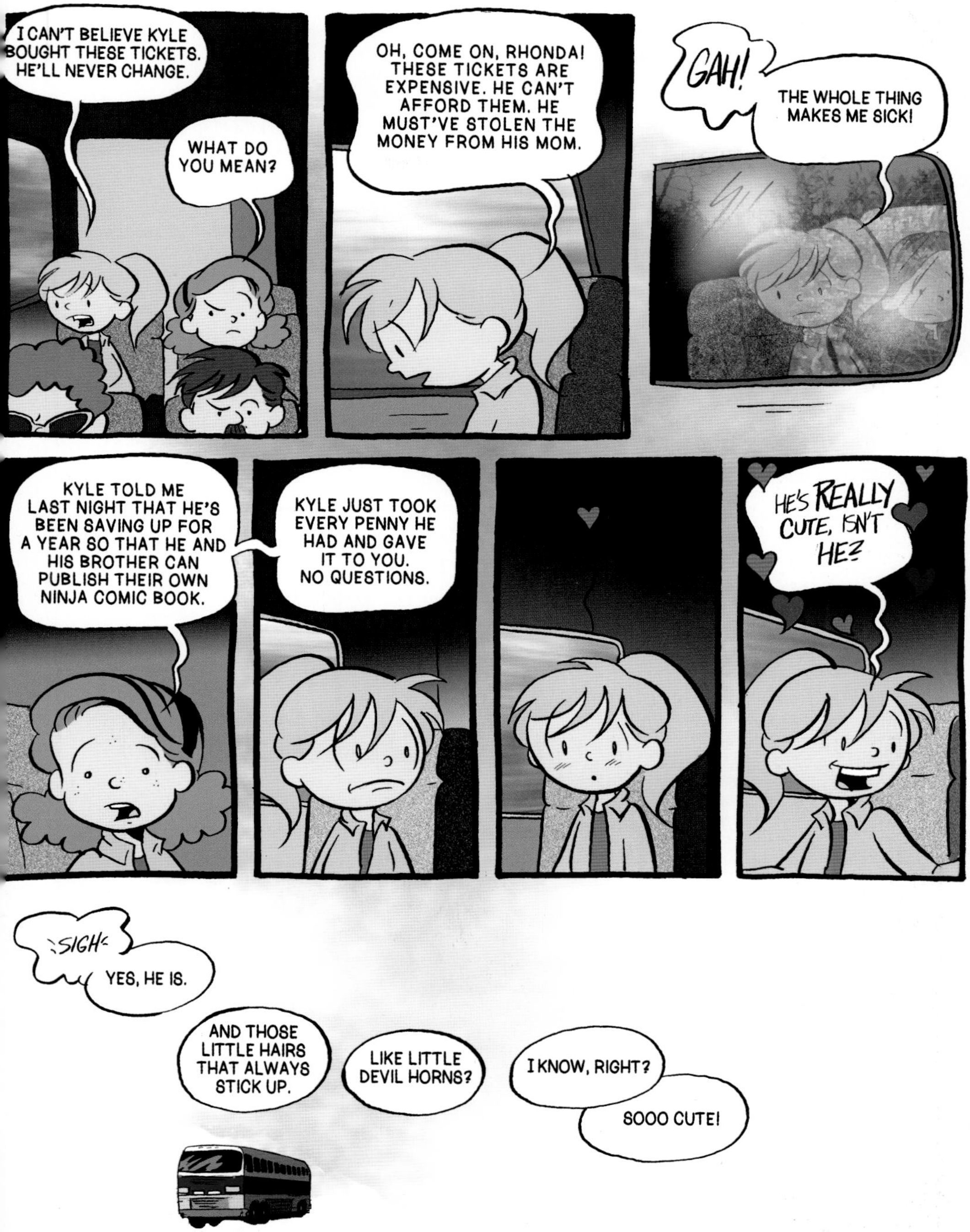
I CAN'T BELIEVE KYLE BOUGHT THESE TICKETS. HE'LL NEVER CHANGE.
WHAT DO YOU MEAN?
OH, COME ON, RHONDA! THESE TICKETS ARE EXPENSIVE. HE CAN'T AFFORD THEM. HE MUST'VE STOLEN THE MONEY FROM HIS MOM.
GAH!
THE WHOLE THING MAKES ME SICK!
KYLE TOLD ME LAST NIGHT THAT HE'S BEEN SAVING UP FOR A YEAR SO THAT HE AND HIS BROTHER CAN PUBLISH THEIR OWN NINJA COMIC BOOK.
KYLE JUST TOOK EVERY PENNY HE HAD AND GAVE IT TO YOU. NO QUESTIONS.
HE'S REALLY CUTE, ISN'T HE?
SIGH
YES, HE IS.
AND THOSE LITTLE HAIRS THAT ALWAYS STICK UP.
LIKE LITTLE DEVIL HORNS?
I KNOW, RIGHT?
SOOO CUTE!

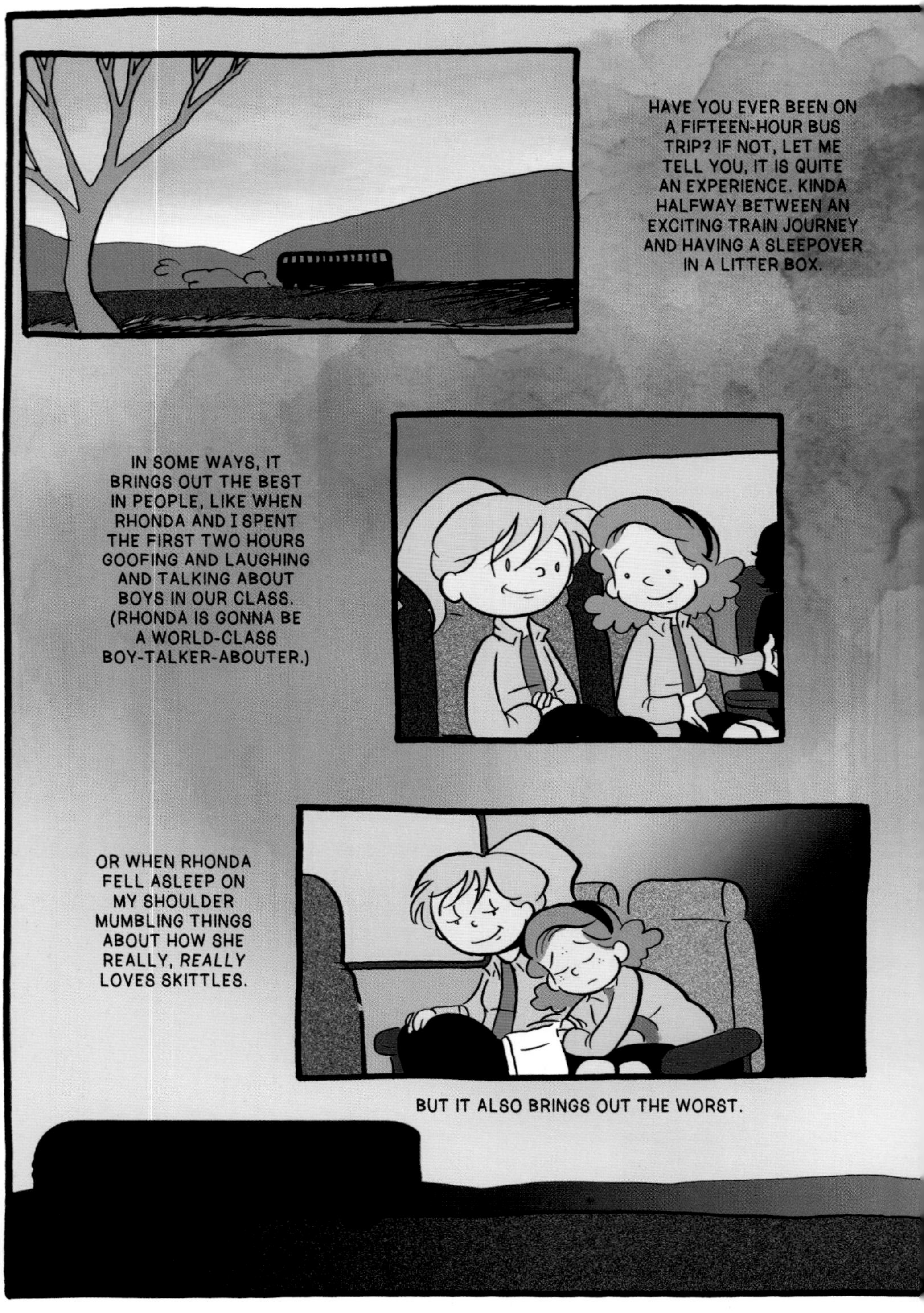
HAVE YOU EVER BEEN ON A FIFTEEN-HOUR BUS TRIP? IF NOT, LET ME TELL YOU, IT IS QUITE AN EXPERIENCE. KINDA HALFWAY BETWEEN AN EXCITING TRAIN JOURNEY AND HAVING A SLEEPOVER IN A LITTER BOX.
IN SOME WAYS, IT BRINGS OUT THE BEST IN PEOPLE, LIKE WHEN RHONDA AND I SPENT THE FIRST TWO HOURS GOOFING AND LAUGHING AND TALKING ABOUT BOYS IN OUR CLASS. (RHONDA IS GONNA BE A WORLD-CLASS BOY-TALKER-ABOUTER.)
OR WHEN RHONDA FELL ASLEEP ON MY SHOULDER MUMBLING THINGS ABOUT HOW SHE REALLY, *REALLY* LOVES SKITTLES.
BUT IT ALSO BRINGS OUT THE WORST.

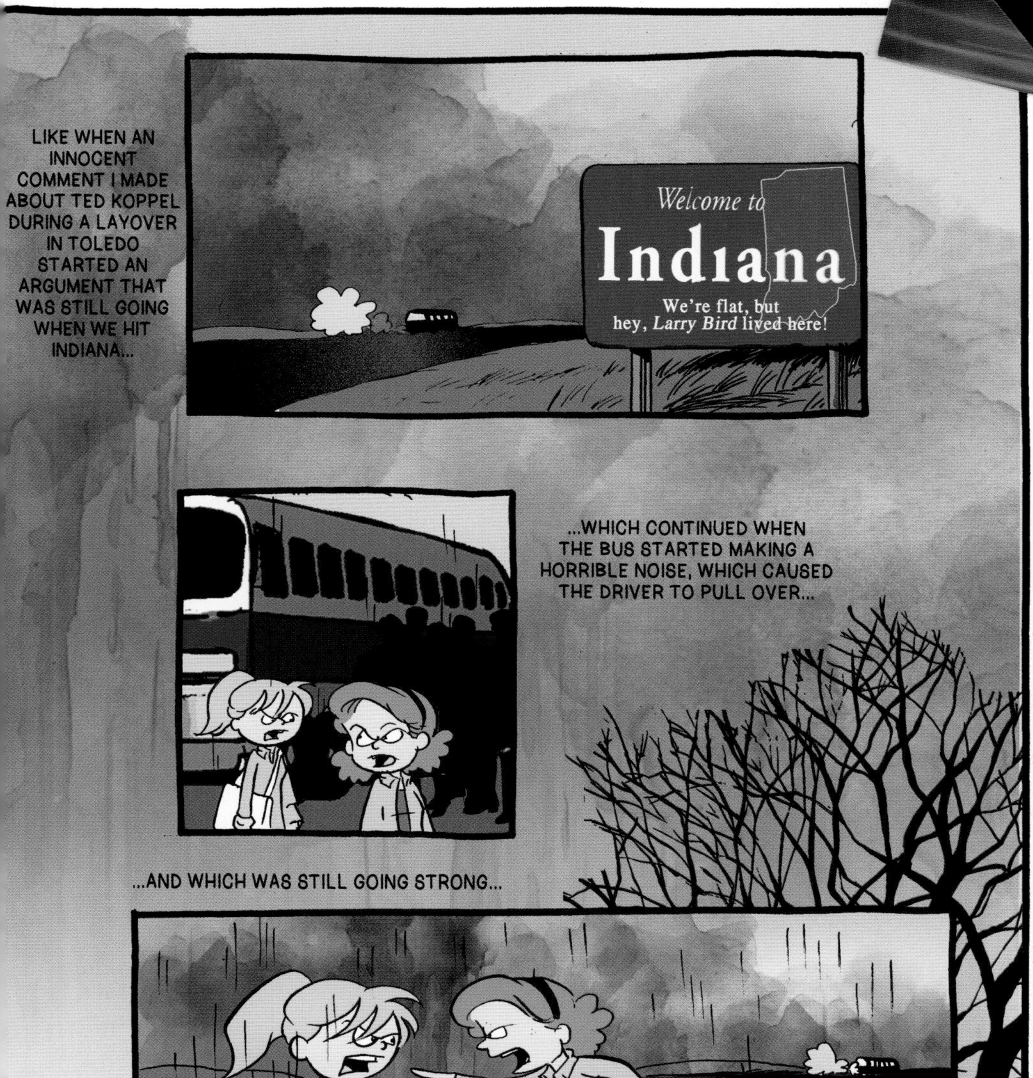
LIKE WHEN AN INNOCENT COMMENT I MADE ABOUT TED KOPPEL DURING A LAYOVER IN TOLEDO STARTED AN ARGUMENT THAT WAS STILL GOING WHEN WE HIT INDIANA...
Welcome to
Indiana
We're flat, but hey, Larry Bird lived here!
...WHICH CONTINUED WHEN THE BUS STARTED MAKING A HORRIBLE NOISE, WHICH CAUSED THE DRIVER TO PULL OVER...
...AND WHICH WAS STILL GOING STRONG...
...WHEN THE DRIVER GAVE THE ALL-CLEAR SIGNAL, AND EVERYONE GOT BACK ON BOARD AND...

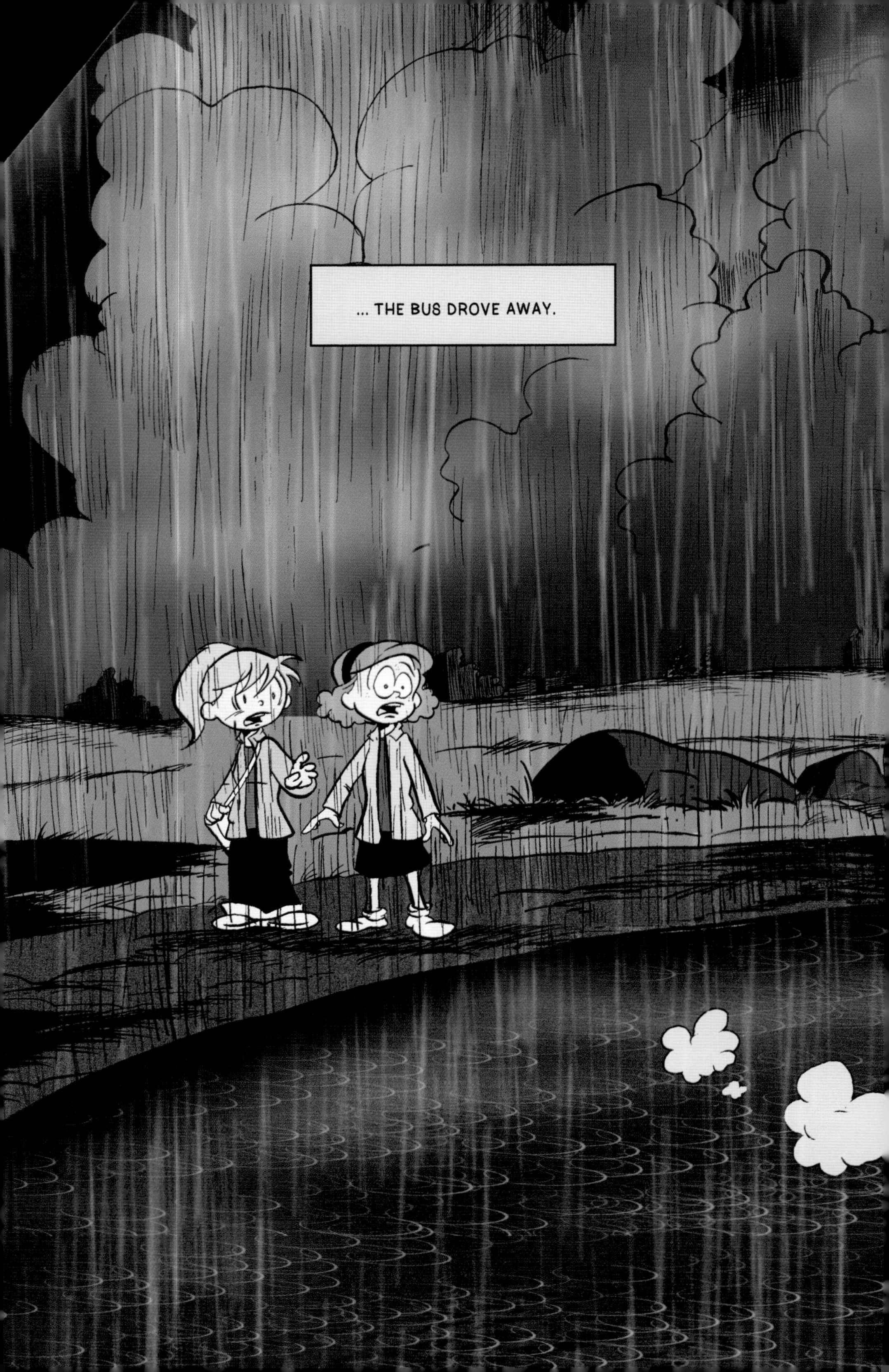
... THE BUS DROVE AWAY.

WHAT *COULD* WE DO?

WE STARTED WALKING.

AND AS WE WALKED, I REMEMBERED A DREAM I'D HAD THE NIGHT BEFORE.

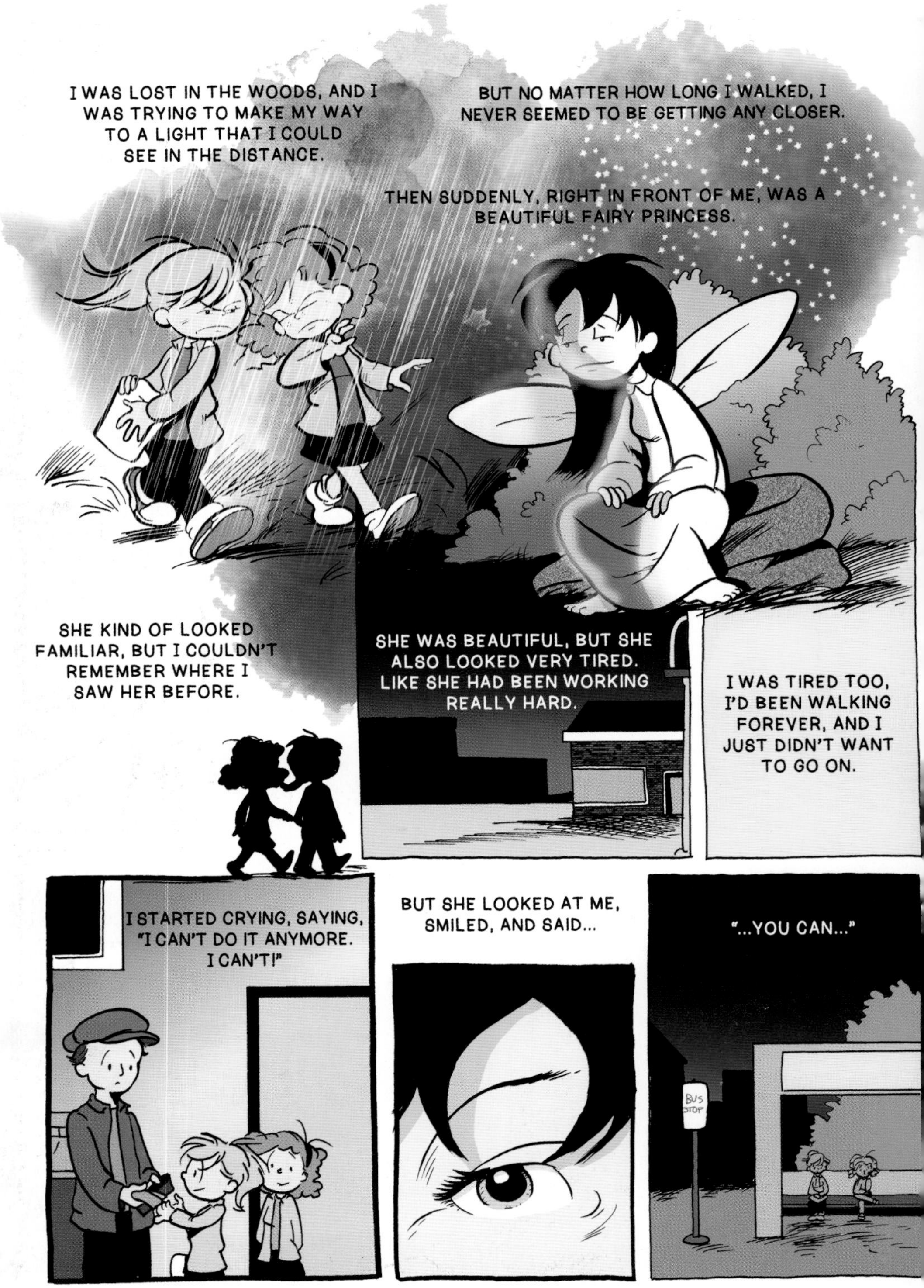
I WAS LOST IN THE WOODS, AND I WAS TRYING TO MAKE MY WAY TO A LIGHT THAT I COULD SEE IN THE DISTANCE.
BUT NO MATTER HOW LONG I WALKED, I NEVER SEEMED TO BE GETTING ANY CLOSER.
THEN SUDDENLY, RIGHT IN FRONT OF ME, WAS A BEAUTIFUL FAIRY PRINCESS.
SHE KIND OF LOOKED FAMILIAR, BUT I COULDN'T REMEMBER WHERE I SAW HER BEFORE.
SHE WAS BEAUTIFUL, BUT SHE ALSO LOOKED VERY TIRED. LIKE SHE HAD BEEN WORKING REALLY HARD.
I WAS TIRED TOO, I'D BEEN WALKING FOREVER, AND I JUST DIDN'T WANT TO GO ON.
I STARTED CRYING, SAYING, "I CAN'T DO IT ANYMORE. I CAN'T!"
BUT SHE LOOKED AT ME, SMILED, AND SAID...
"...YOU CAN..."
BUS STOP

".. BECAUSE YOU HAVE TO."

WOW, I CAN'T BELIEVE THEY ALL ACTUALLY SHOWED UP!

THERE ARE DOZENS OF 'EM!

AND DID WE GET GOOD TESTIMONIALS?

YEP, AND SAM IS UPLOADING THEM NOW.

PERFECT.

YOU GUYS KNOW THE PLAN?

I KNOW IT'S STUPID.

WELL, THAT'S THE DIFFERENCE BETWEEN US, KYLE. YOU SEE THE GLASS AS HALF EMPTY.

...AND I SEE YOU AS A JERK.

GUYS.

NO TIME TO ARGUE.

IT'S SHOWTIME.

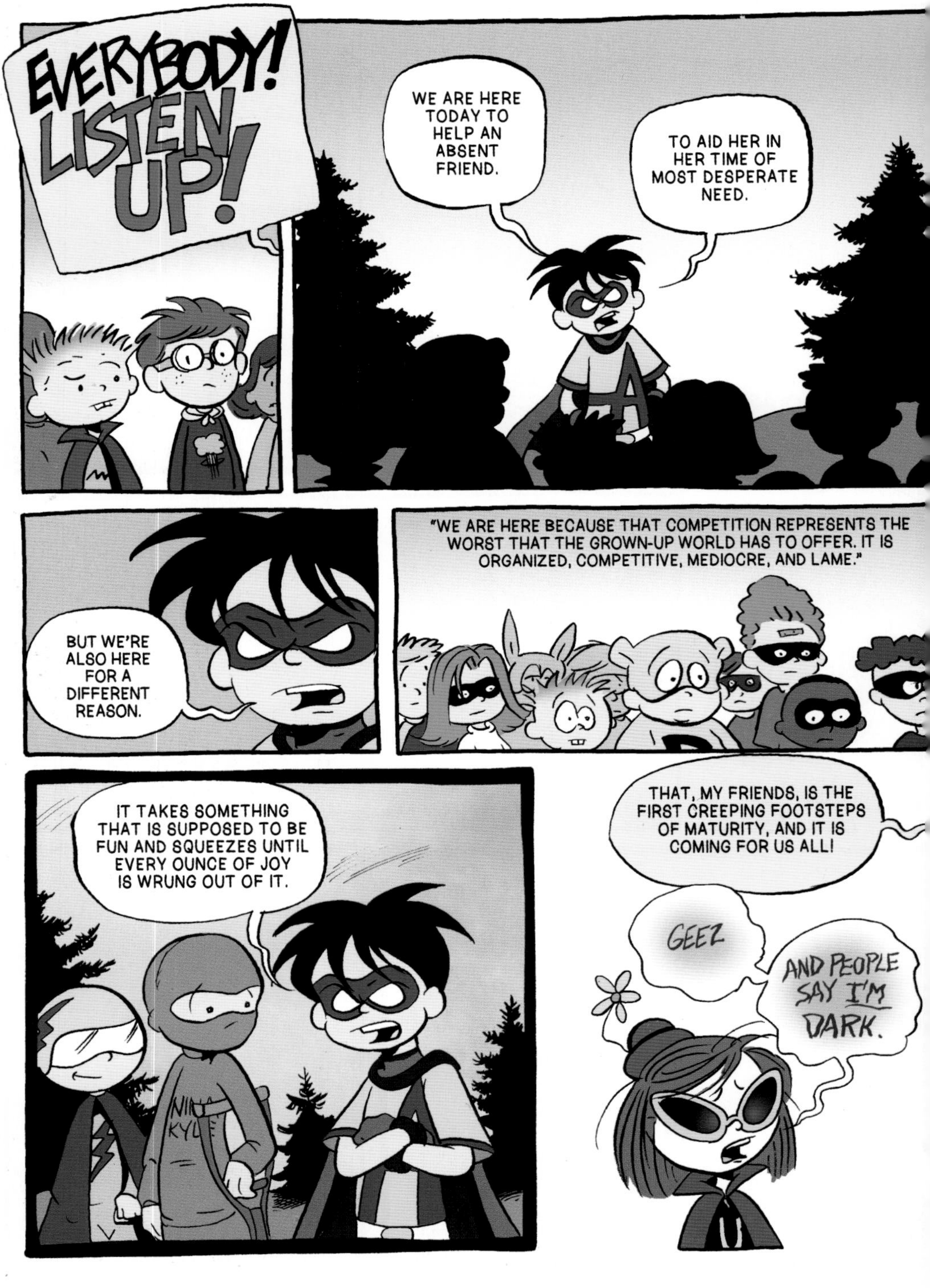
EVERYBODY! LISTEN UP!
WE ARE HERE TODAY TO HELP AN ABSENT FRIEND.
TO AID HER IN HER TIME OF MOST DESPERATE NEED.
BUT WE'RE ALSO HERE FOR A DIFFERENT REASON.
"WE ARE HERE BECAUSE THAT COMPETITION REPRESENTS THE WORST THAT THE GROWN-UP WORLD HAS TO OFFER. IT IS ORGANIZED, COMPETITIVE, MEDIOCRE, AND LAME."
IT TAKES SOMETHING THAT IS SUPPOSED TO BE FUN AND SQUEEZES UNTIL EVERY OUNCE OF JOY IS WRUNG OUT OF IT.
THAT, MY FRIENDS, IS THE FIRST CREEPING FOOTSTEPS OF MATURITY, AND IT IS COMING FOR US ALL!
GEEZ
AND PEOPLE SAY I'M DARK.

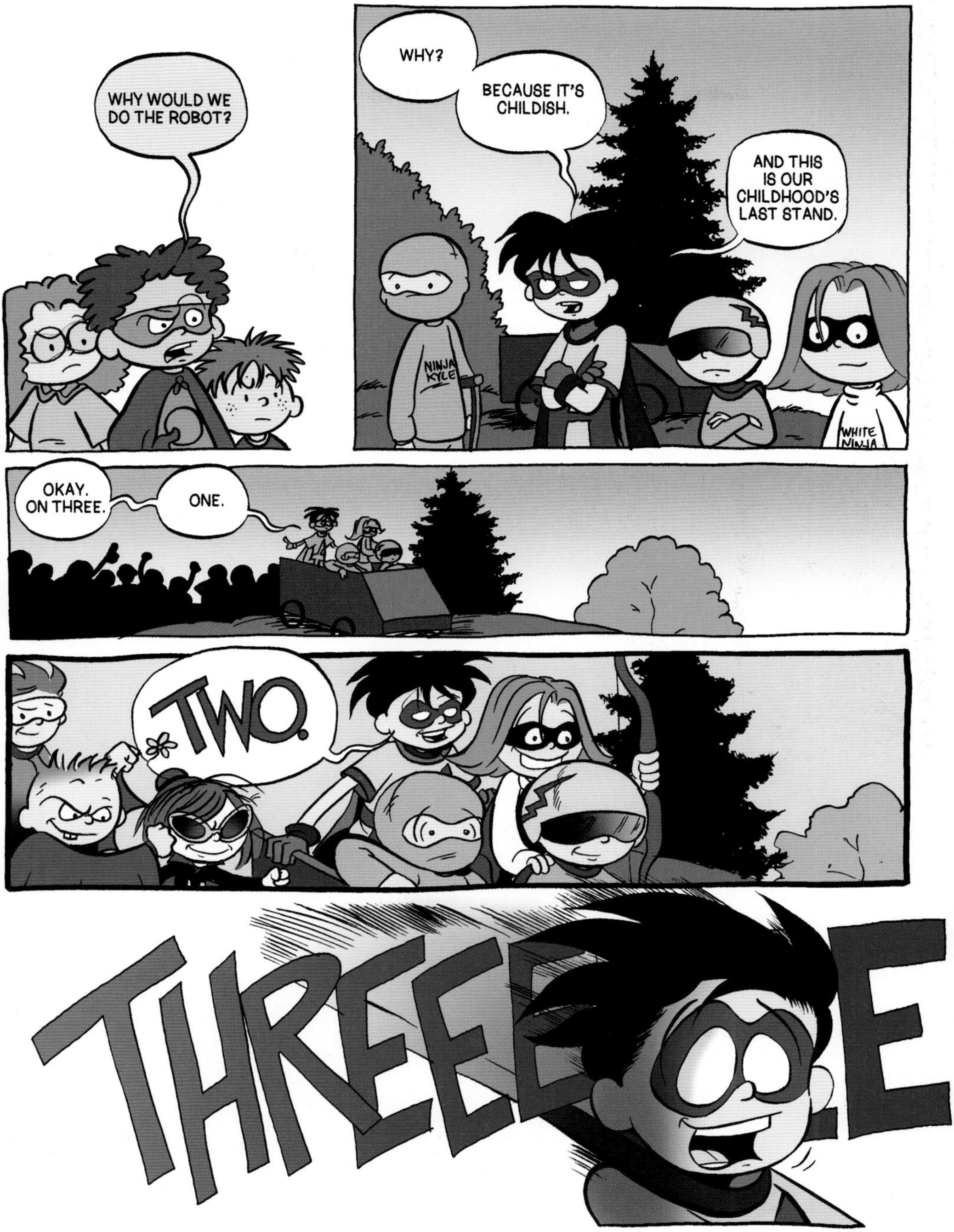

WHY WOULD WE DO THE ROBOT?
WHY?
BECAUSE IT'S CHILDISH.
AND THIS IS OUR CHILDHOOD'S LAST STAND.
NINJA KYLE
WHITE NINJA
OKAY. ON THREE.
ONE.
TWO.
THREEEEE

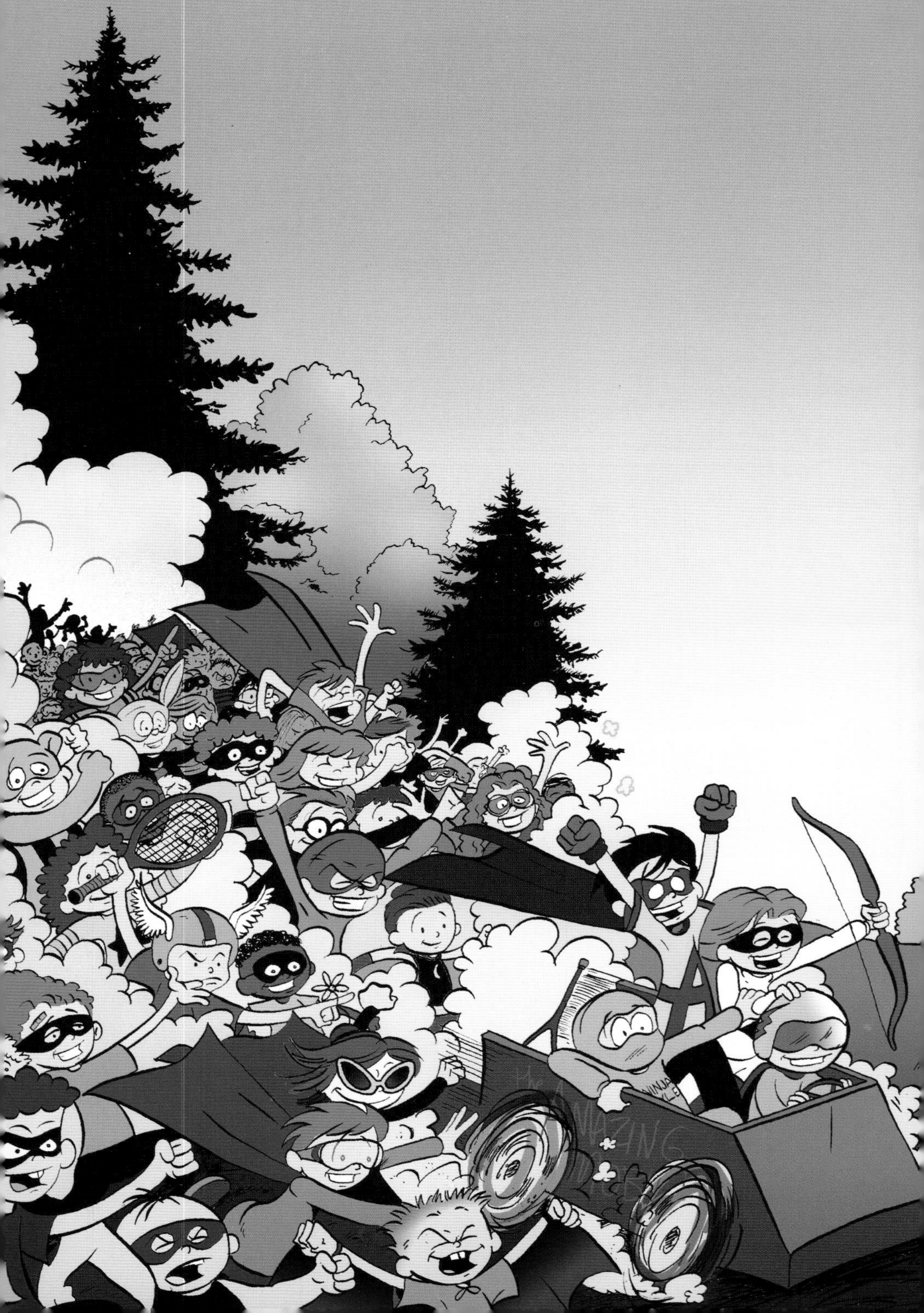
NINJA

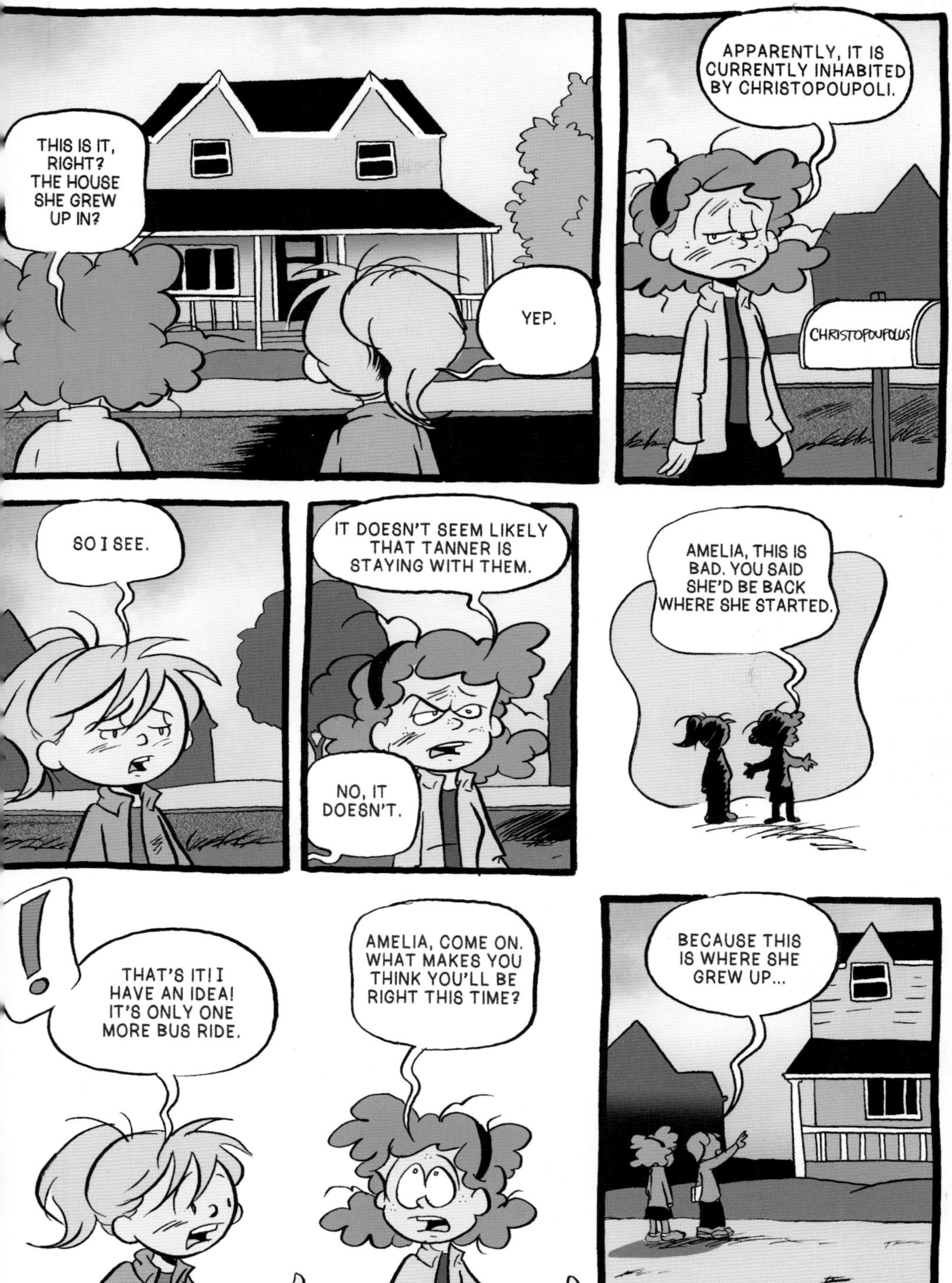
THIS IS IT, RIGHT? THE HOUSE SHE GREW UP IN?
YEP.
APPARENTLY, IT IS CURRENTLY INHABITED BY CHRISTOPOUPOLI.
CHRISTOPOUPOLUS
SO I SEE.
IT DOESN'T SEEM LIKELY THAT TANNER IS STAYING WITH THEM.
NO, IT DOESN'T.
AMELIA, THIS IS BAD. YOU SAID SHE'D BE BACK WHERE SHE STARTED.
!
THAT'S IT! I HAVE AN IDEA! IT'S ONLY ONE MORE BUS RIDE.
AMELIA, COME ON. WHAT MAKES YOU THINK YOU'LL BE RIGHT THIS TIME?
BECAUSE THIS IS WHERE SHE GREW UP...

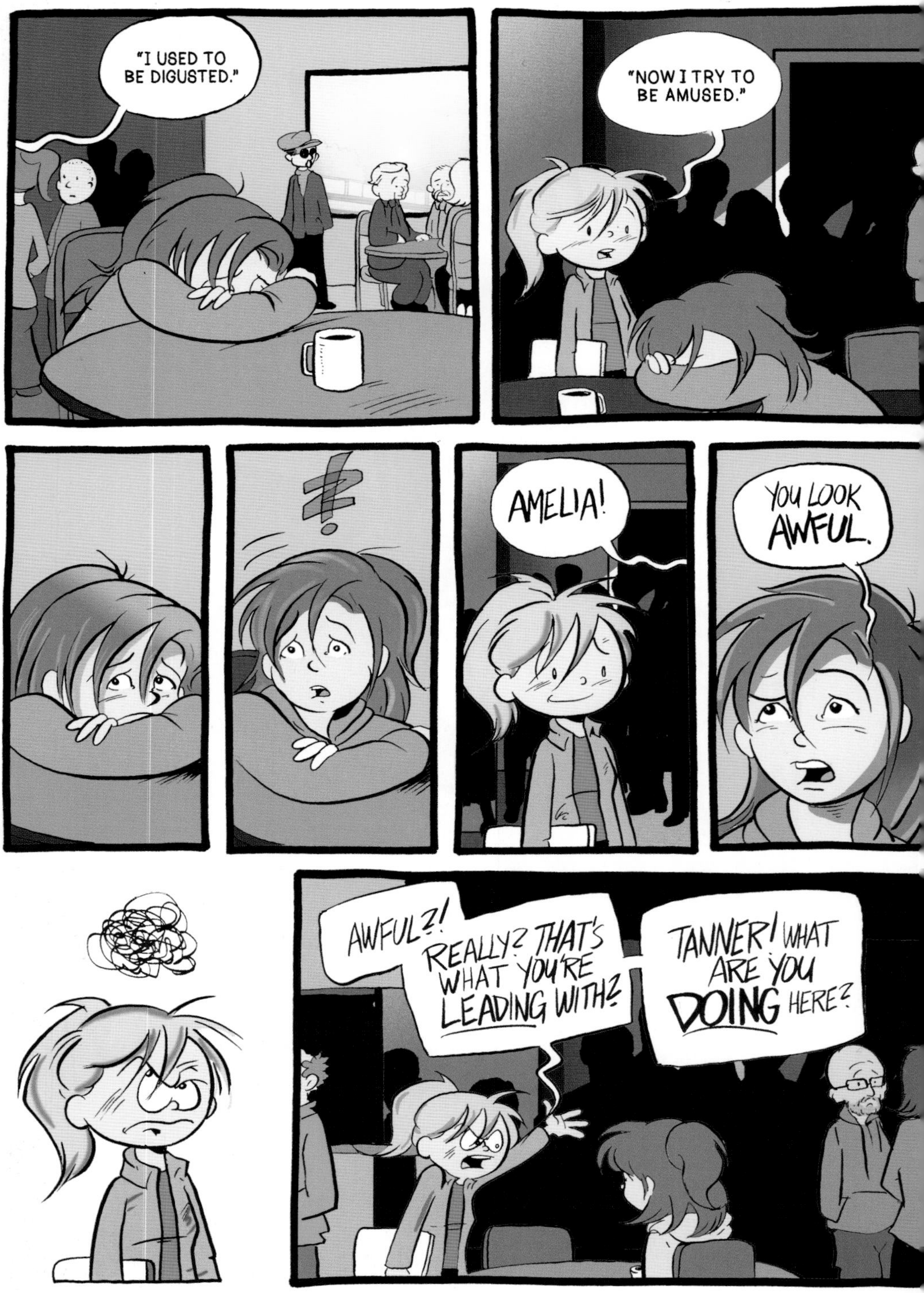
"I USED TO BE DIGUSTED."
"NOW I TRY TO BE AMUSED."
AMELIA!
YOU LOOK AWFUL.
AWFUL?! REALLY? THAT'S WHAT YOU'RE LEADING WITH?
TANNER! WHAT ARE YOU DOING HERE?

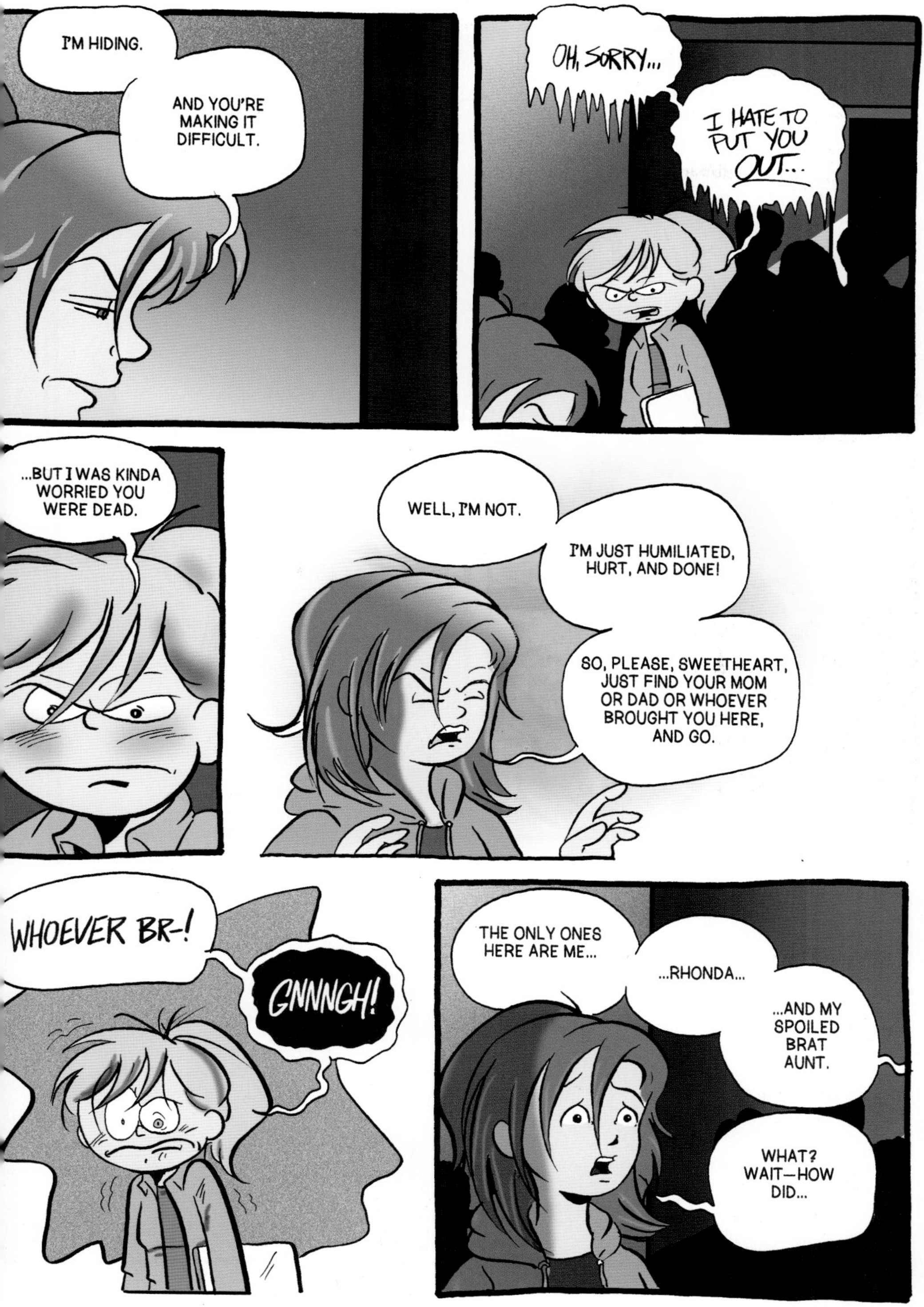
I'M HIDING.
AND YOU'RE MAKING IT DIFFICULT.
OH, SORRY...
I HATE TO PUT YOU OUT...
...BUT I WAS KINDA WORRIED YOU WERE DEAD.
WELL, I'M NOT.
I'M JUST HUMILIATED, HURT, AND DONE!
SO, PLEASE, SWEETHEART, JUST FIND YOUR MOM OR DAD OR WHOEVER BROUGHT YOU HERE, AND GO.
WHOEVER BR-!
GNNNGH!
THE ONLY ONES HERE ARE ME...
...RHONDA...
...AND MY SPOILED BRAT AUNT.
WHAT? WAIT—HOW DID...

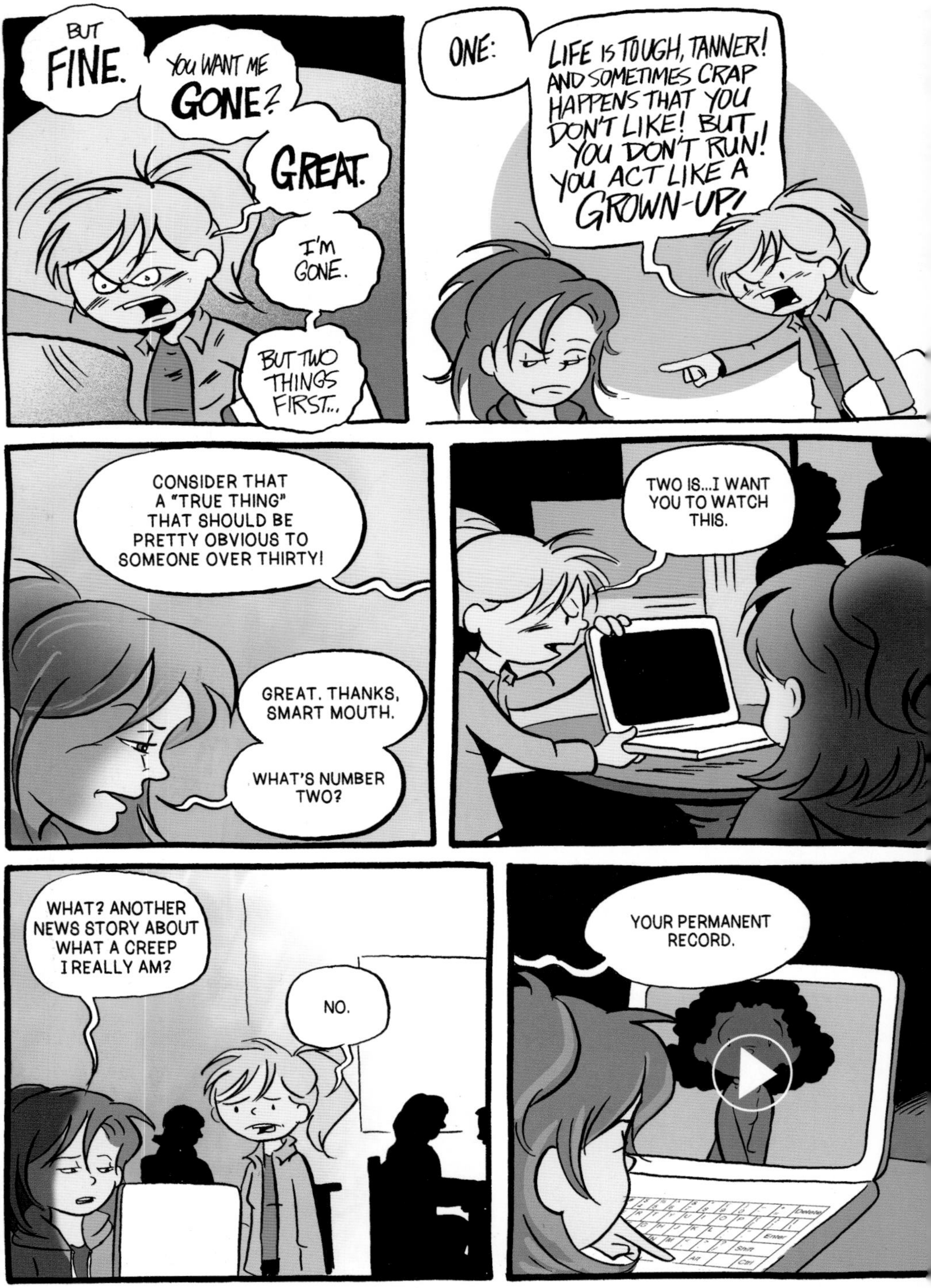
BUT FINE.
YOU WANT ME GONE?
GREAT.
I'M GONE.
BUT TWO THINGS FIRST...
ONE:
LIFE IS TOUGH, TANNER! AND SOMETIMES CRAP HAPPENS THAT YOU DON'T LIKE! BUT YOU DON'T RUN! YOU ACT LIKE A GROWN-UP!
CONSIDER THAT A "TRUE THING" THAT SHOULD BE PRETTY OBVIOUS TO SOMEONE OVER THIRTY!
GREAT. THANKS, SMART MOUTH.
WHAT'S NUMBER TWO?
TWO IS...I WANT YOU TO WATCH THIS.
WHAT? ANOTHER NEWS STORY ABOUT WHAT A CREEP I REALLY AM?
NO.
YOUR PERMANENT RECORD.

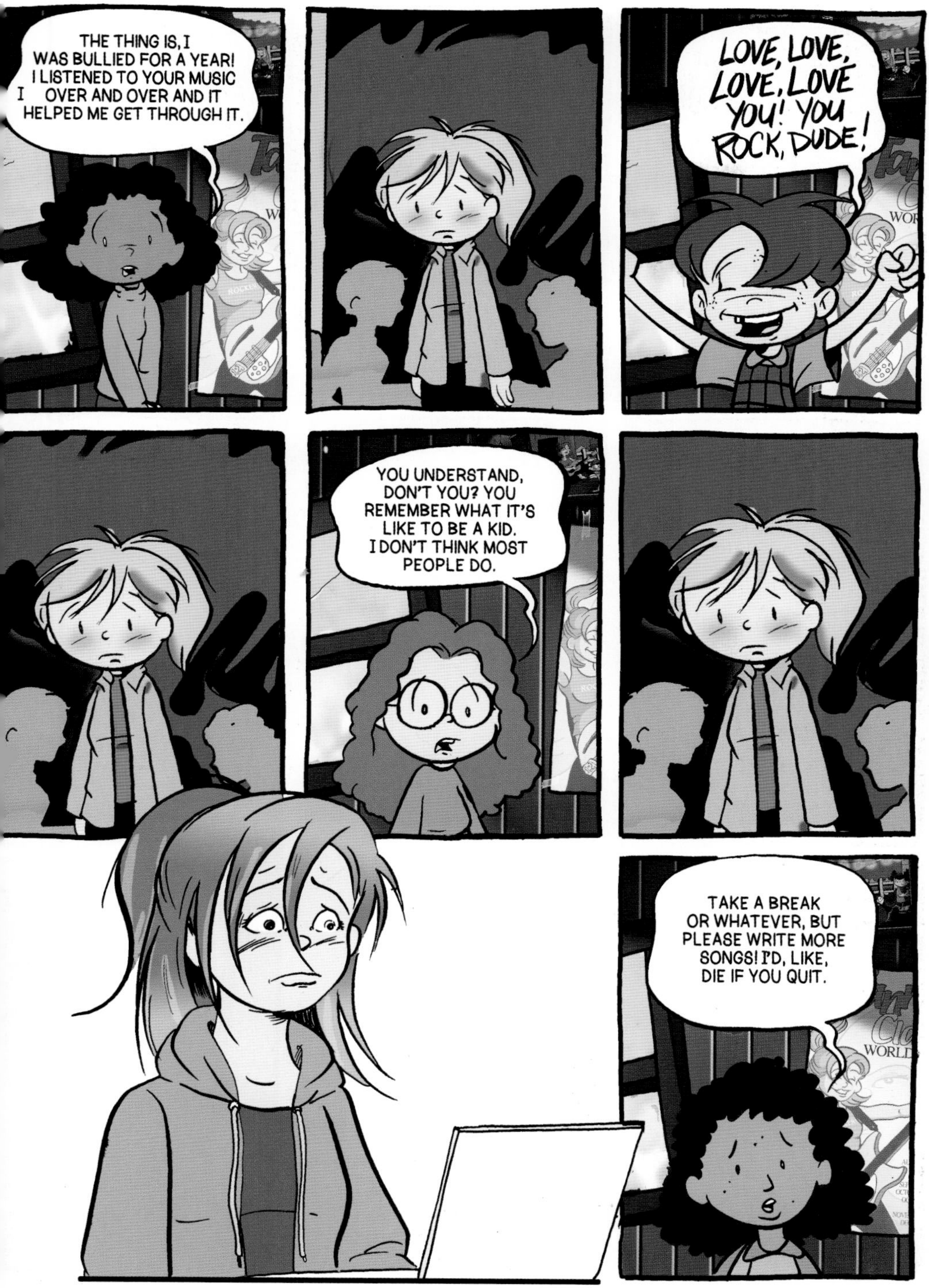
THE THING IS, I WAS BULLIED FOR A YEAR! I LISTENED TO YOUR MUSIC OVER AND OVER AND IT HELPED ME GET THROUGH IT.
LOVE, LOVE, LOVE, LOVE YOU! YOU ROCK, DUDE!
YOU UNDERSTAND, DON'T YOU? YOU REMEMBER WHAT IT'S LIKE TO BE A KID. I DON'T THINK MOST PEOPLE DO.
TAKE A BREAK OR WHATEVER, BUT PLEASE WRITE MORE SONGS! I'D, LIKE, DIE IF YOU QUIT.

133

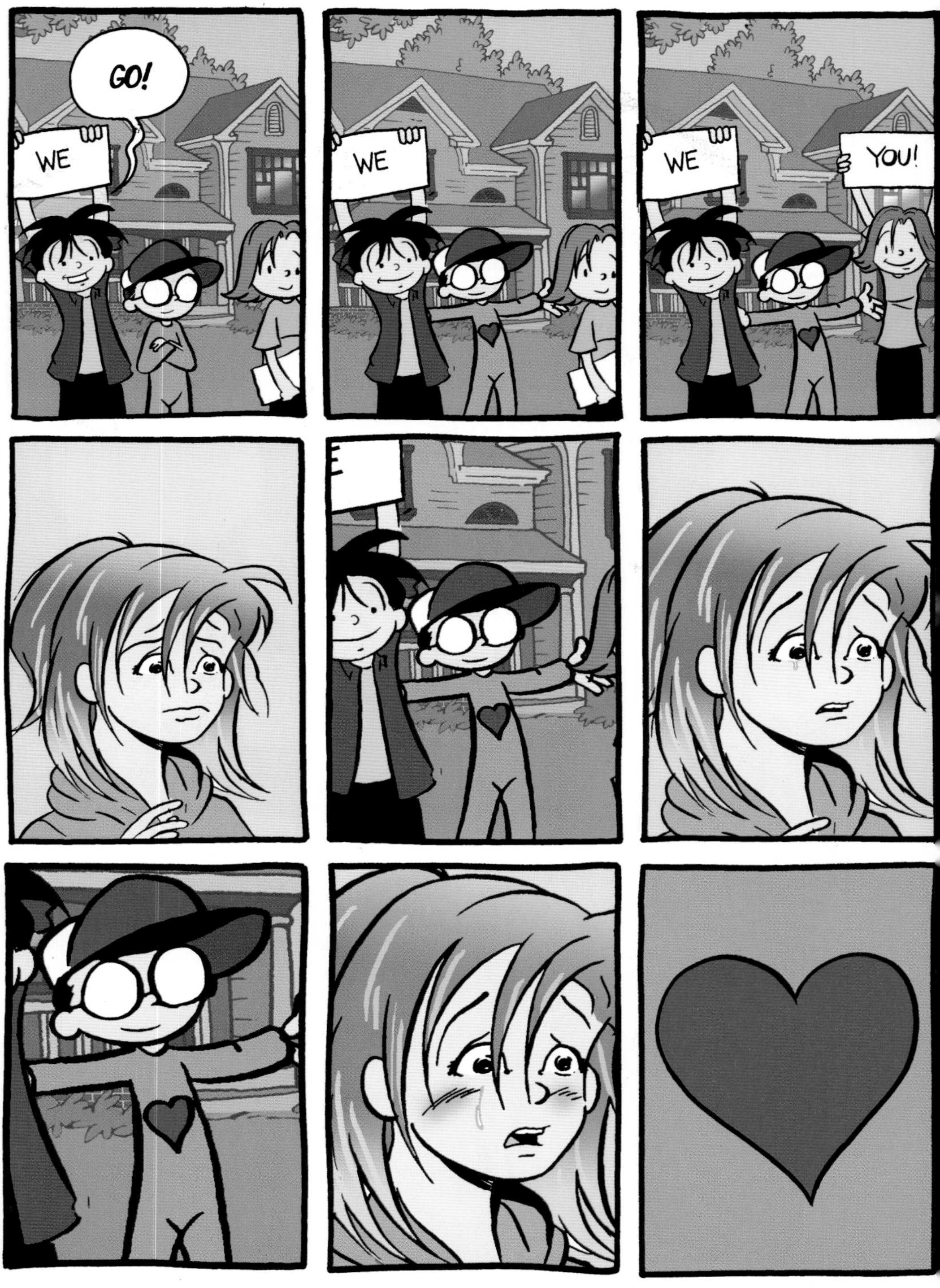
GO!
WE
WE
WE
YOU!

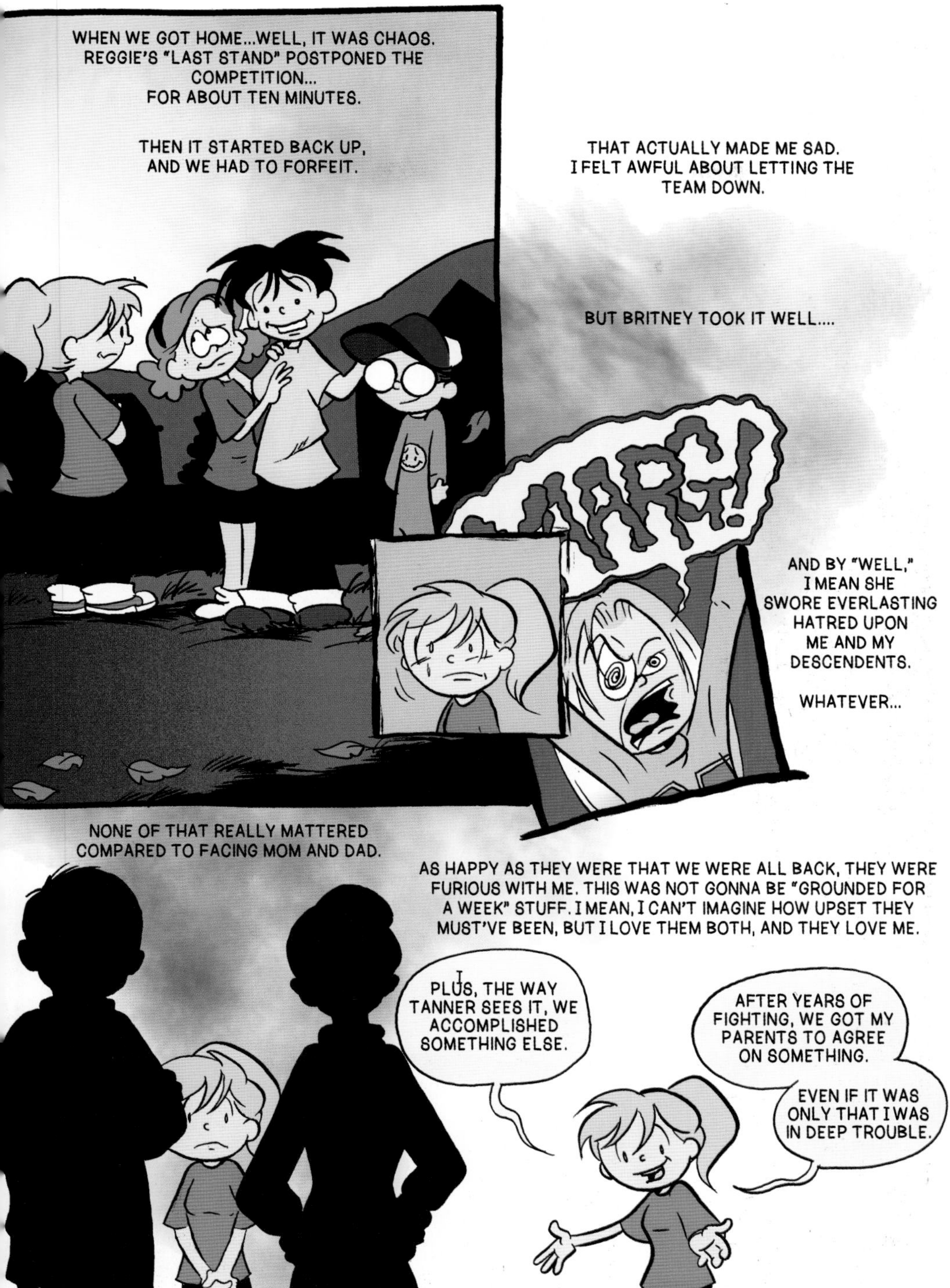
WHEN WE GOT HOME...WELL, IT WAS CHAOS. REGGIE'S "LAST STAND" POSTPONED THE COMPETITION... FOR ABOUT TEN MINUTES.
THEN IT STARTED BACK UP, AND WE HAD TO FORFEIT.
THAT ACTUALLY MADE ME SAD. I FELT AWFUL ABOUT LETTING THE TEAM DOWN.
BUT BRITNEY TOOK IT WELL....
ARG!
AND BY "WELL," I MEAN SHE SWORE EVERLASTING HATRED UPON ME AND MY DESCENDENTS.
WHATEVER...
NONE OF THAT REALLY MATTERED COMPARED TO FACING MOM AND DAD.
AS HAPPY AS THEY WERE THAT WE WERE ALL BACK, THEY WERE FURIOUS WITH ME. THIS WAS NOT GONNA BE "GROUNDED FOR A WEEK" STUFF. I MEAN, I CAN'T IMAGINE HOW UPSET THEY MUST'VE BEEN, BUT I LOVE THEM BOTH, AND THEY LOVE ME.
PLUS, THE WAY TANNER SEES IT, WE ACCOMPLISHED SOMETHING ELSE.
AFTER YEARS OF FIGHTING, WE GOT MY PARENTS TO AGREE ON SOMETHING.
EVEN IF IT WAS ONLY THAT I WAS IN DEEP TROUBLE.

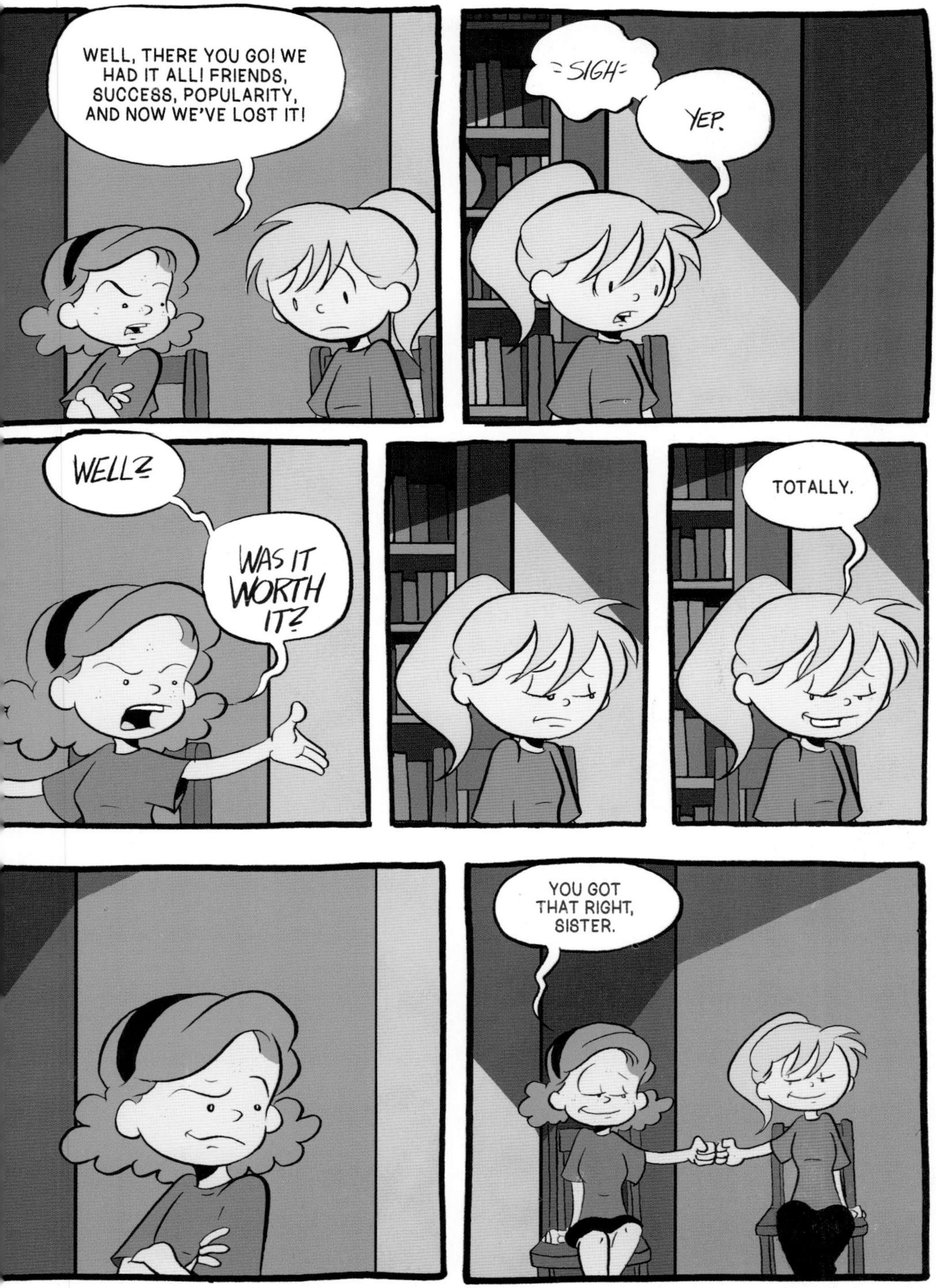
WELL, THERE YOU GO! WE HAD IT ALL! FRIENDS, SUCCESS, POPULARITY, AND NOW WE'VE LOST IT!
=SIGH=
YEP.
WELL?
WAS IT WORTH IT?
TOTALLY.
YOU GOT THAT RIGHT, SISTER.

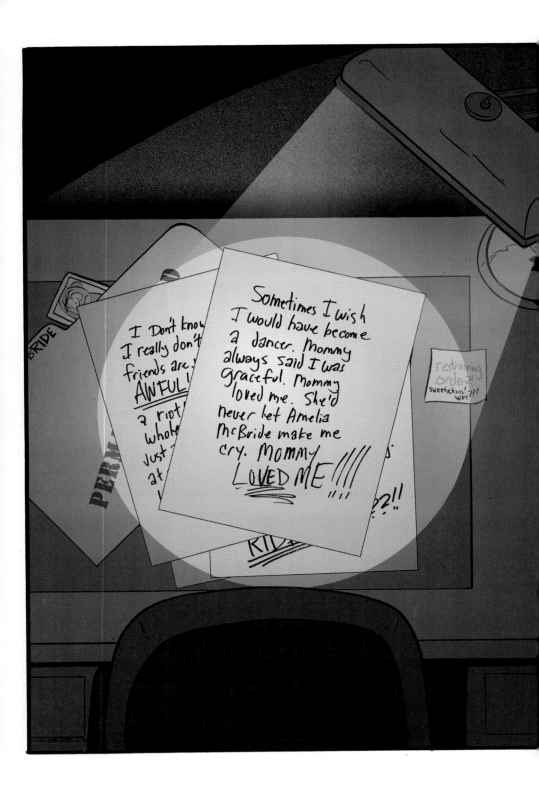

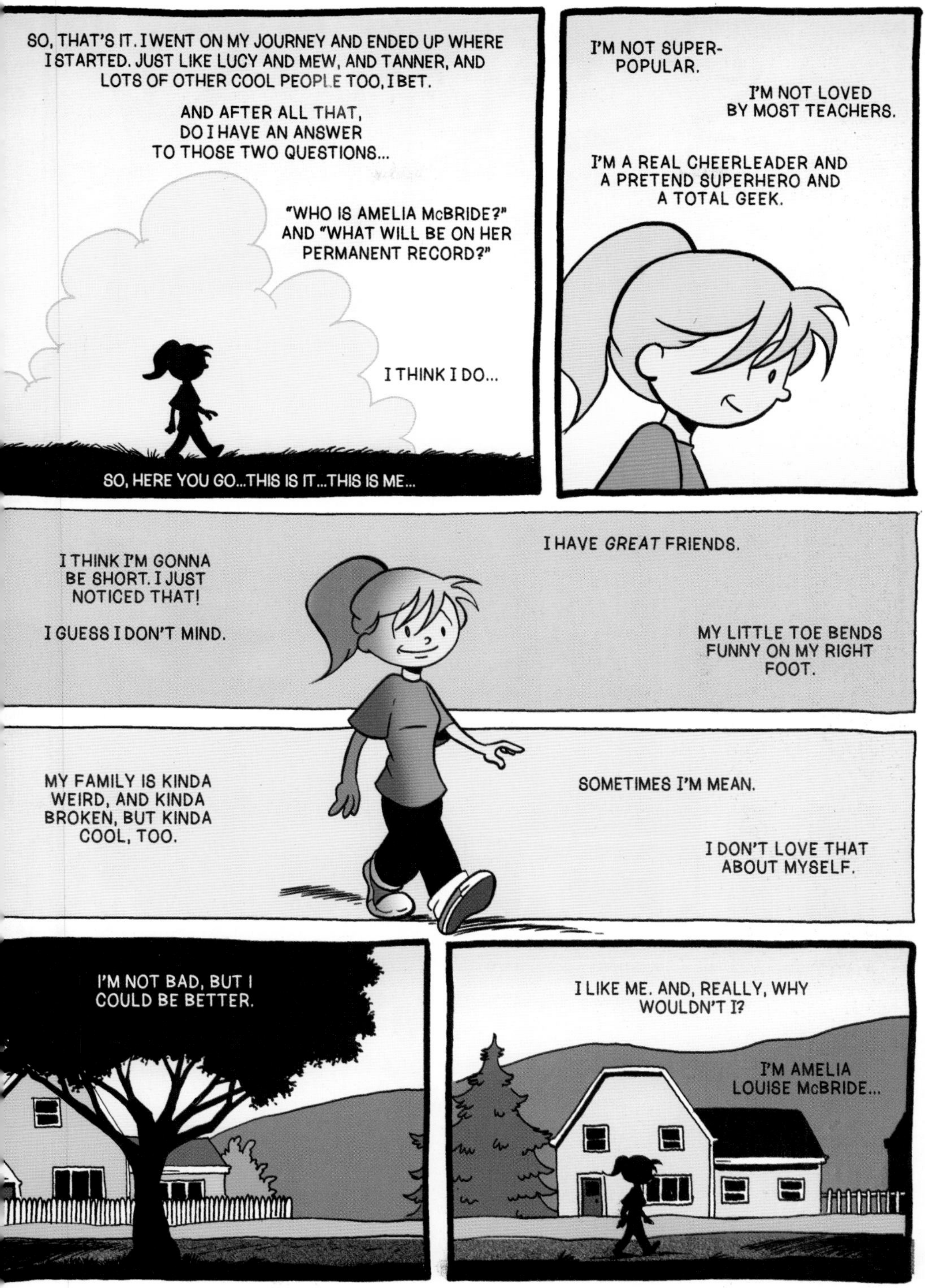

SO, THAT'S IT. I WENT ON MY JOURNEY AND ENDED UP WHERE I STARTED. JUST LIKE LUCY AND MEW, AND TANNER, AND LOTS OF OTHER COOL PEOPLE TOO, I BET.
AND AFTER ALL THAT, DO I HAVE AN ANSWER TO THOSE TWO QUESTIONS...
"WHO IS AMELIA McBRIDE?" AND "WHAT WILL BE ON HER PERMANENT RECORD?"
I THINK I DO...
SO, HERE YOU GO...THIS IS IT...THIS IS ME...
I'M NOT SUPER-POPULAR.
I'M NOT LOVED BY MOST TEACHERS.
I'M A REAL CHEERLEADER AND A PRETEND SUPERHERO AND A TOTAL GEEK.
I THINK I'M GONNA BE SHORT. I JUST NOTICED THAT!
I GUESS I DON'T MIND.
I HAVE *GREAT* FRIENDS.
MY LITTLE TOE BENDS FUNNY ON MY RIGHT FOOT.
MY FAMILY IS KINDA WEIRD, AND KINDA BROKEN, BUT KINDA COOL, TOO.
SOMETIMES I'M MEAN.
I DON'T LOVE THAT ABOUT MYSELF.
I'M NOT BAD, BUT I COULD BE BETTER.
I LIKE ME. AND, REALLY, WHY WOULDN'T I?
I'M AMELIA LOUISE McBRIDE...

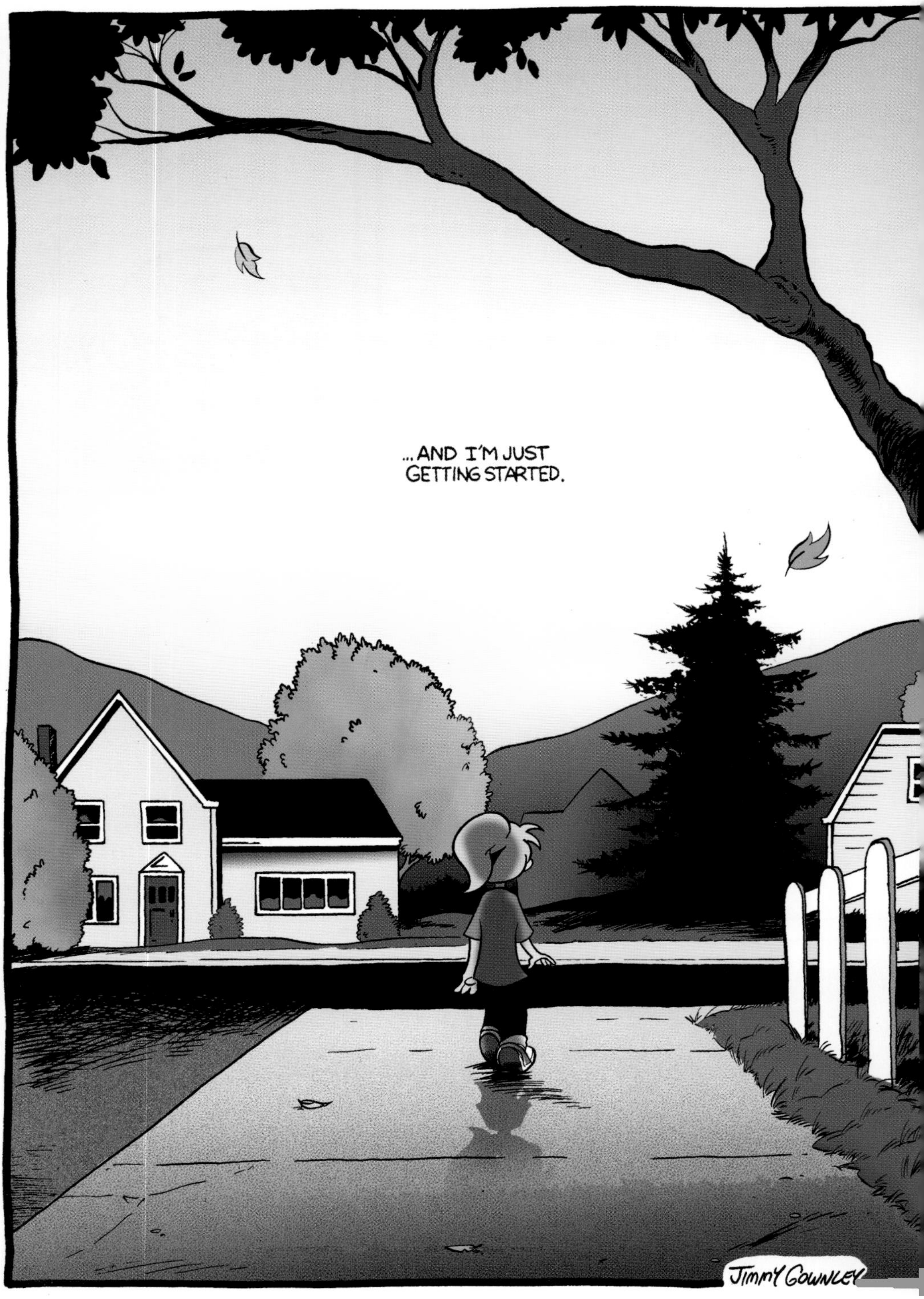
...AND I'M JUST
GETTING STARTED.
JIMMY GOWNLEY

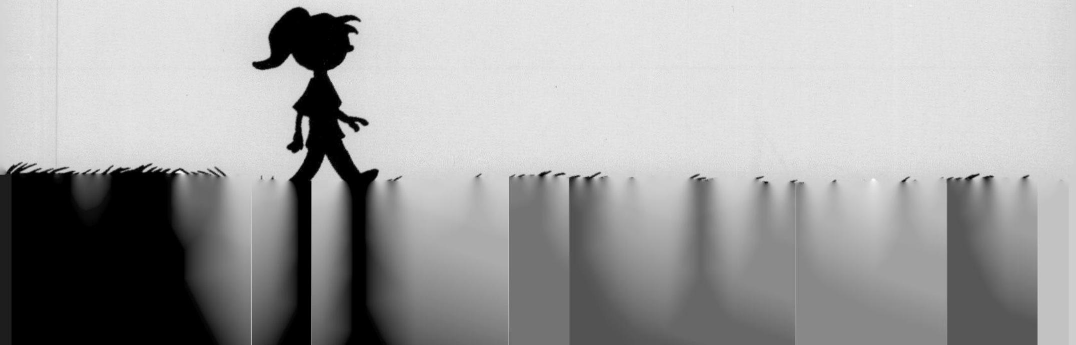

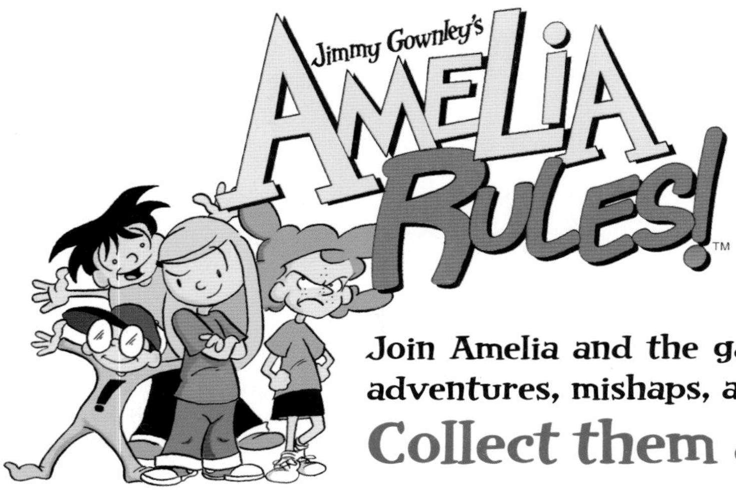

Jimmy Gownley's
AMELIA RULES!™

Join Amelia and the gang for adventures, mishaps, and homework.

Collect them all!

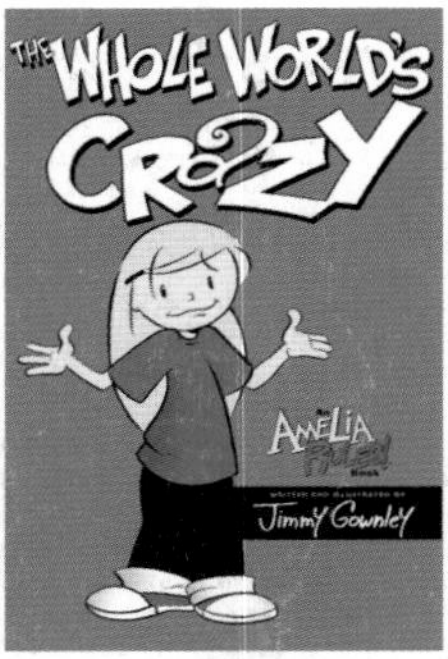

THE WHOLE WORLD'S CRAZY
AMELIA RULES!
Jimmy Gownley

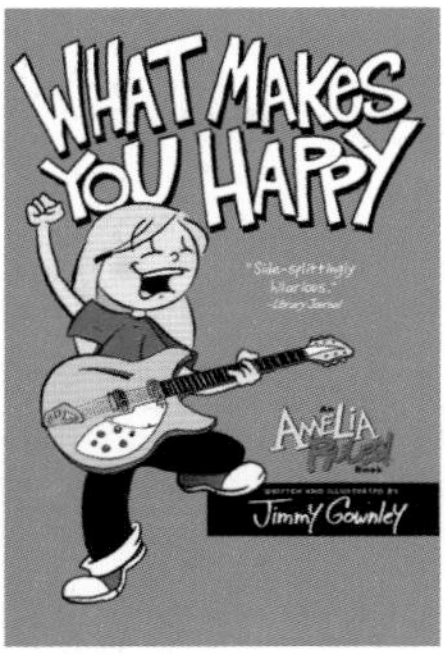

WHAT MAKES YOU HAPPY
AMELIA RULES!
Jimmy Gownley

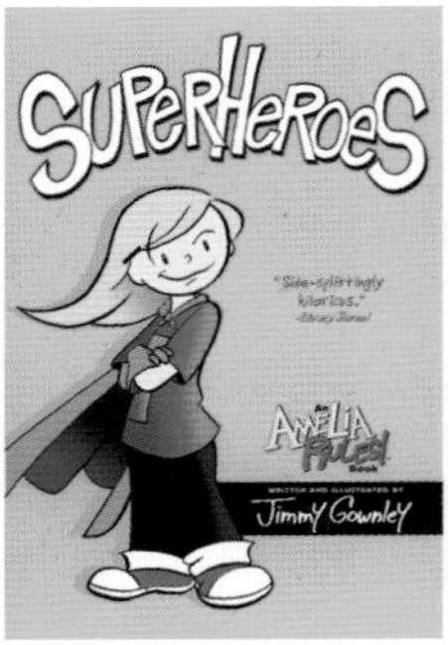

SUPERHEROES
AMELIA RULES!
Jimmy Gownley

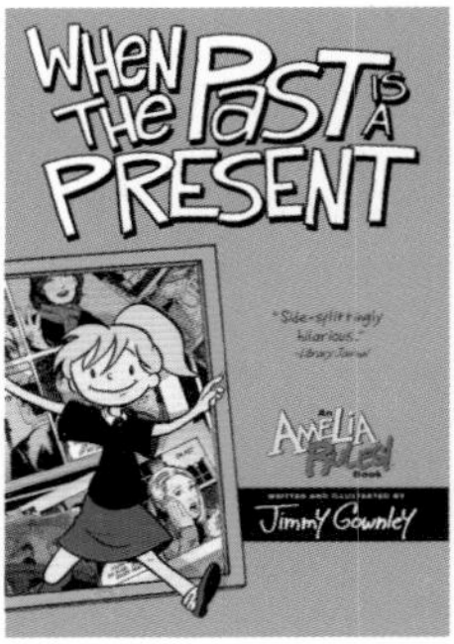

WHEN THE PAST IS A PRESENT
AMELIA RULES!
Jimmy Gownley

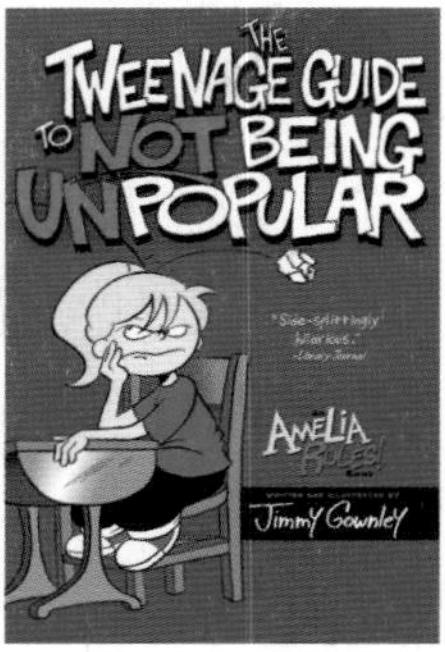

THE TWEENAGE GUIDE TO NOT BEING UNPOPULAR
AMELIA RULES!
Jimmy Gownley

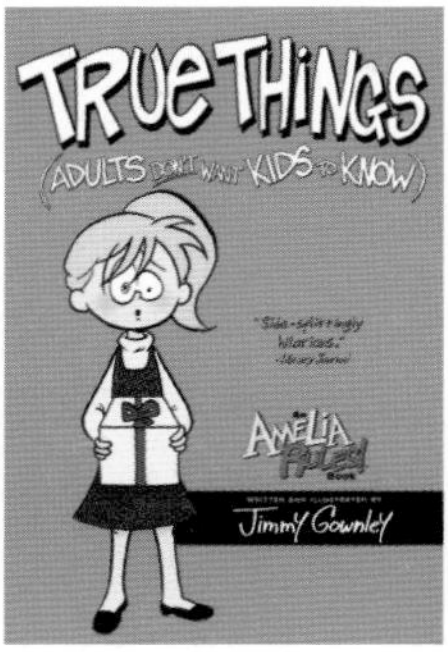

TRUE THINGS
(ADULTS DON'T WANT KIDS TO KNOW)
AMELIA RULES!
Jimmy Gownley

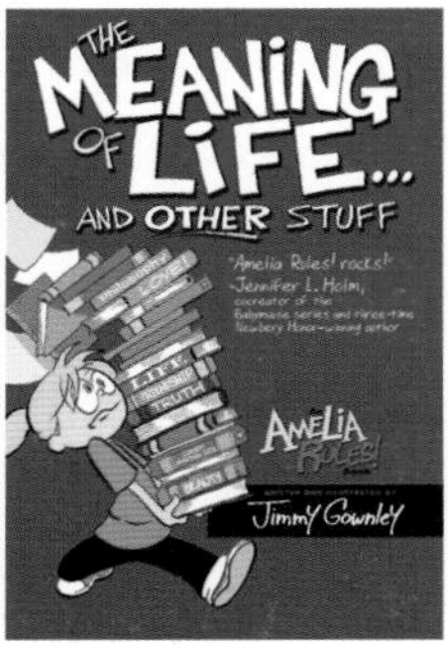

THE MEANING OF LIFE... AND OTHER STUFF
"Amelia Rules! rocks!"
-Jennifer L. Holm
AMELIA RULES!
Jimmy Gownley

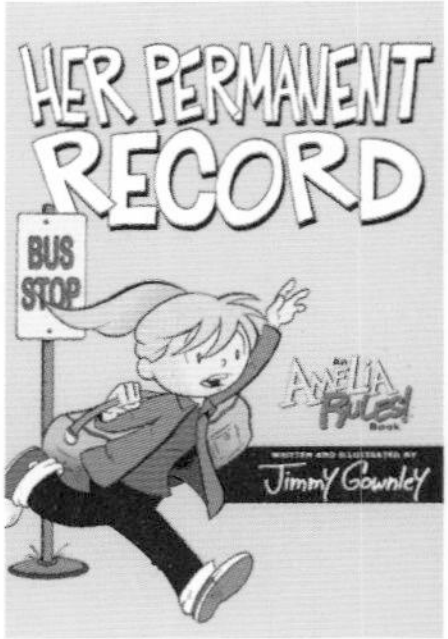

HER PERMANENT RECORD
BUS STOP
AMELIA RULES!
Jimmy Gownley

atheneum

From Atheneum Books for Young Readers

KIDS.SimonandSchuster.com